The Candle Flame

by

Mirabelle Maslin

Augur Press

THE CANDLE FLAME
Copyright © Mirabelle Maslin 2009

The moral right of the author has been asserted

Author of:
Beyond the Veil
Tracy
Carl and other writings
Fay
On a Dog Lead
Emily
The Fifth Key

British Library Cataloguing in Publication Data.
A catalogue record for this book is available from the British Library.

ISBN 978-0-9558936-1-2

First published 2009 by
Augur Press
Delf House,
52, Penicuik Road,
Roslin,
Midlothian EH25 9LH
United Kingdom

Printed by Lightning Source

The Candle Flame

With thanks to all who value my work

Chapter One

She sat watching the yellow flame from a roughly made candle that was positioned in the middle of the table. There had been little movement for a long time, but now it fluttered to one side, and she knew that something must have happened. There was no other source of light, as the fire in the hearth was laid but not lit – waiting for the return of the men. Her acute hearing had not picked up anything. Yet there must be something. She felt the hairs on the back of her neck begin to prickle, and she froze, barely breathing, concentrating every sense upon the task of identifying the source of the change.

Scanning the shadows, she could detect nothing. She longed to turn her head, but instinctively she knew that she must not. Then she thought that she might have heard a tiny creaking sound. She strained her ears, and at the same time picked up a minute change in the air around her right shoulder, from which her shawl had slipped, revealing bare skin. Her fingers seemed to turn to icicles as her body closed down in an attempt to shield itself from the unknown menace that, although barely perceptible to her physical senses, threatened to pervade her soul.

The passage of time was measured only by the slow shortening of the candle that was her companion on this dark winter day. How much longer before the others returned? Her tortured mind could not guess. Had she been alone, she would have lit a second candle before the first collapsed and died. But she knew that an invisible entity had filled the room, and she dared not stir. No sound, nothing visible, yet she knew that she was being observed, minutely, and her only defence was to remain as still as the solid wooden table upon which she leaned.

Concentrating every inner resource upon this task, another burden began to weigh on her. The height of the candle told her that it had little life remaining. The flame moved again, and she forced herself to suppress a shudder. Terrible though it was to be in this position, the condition she imagined once the candle had died was untenable.

The candle sunk ever lower, its flame now remaining surprisingly steady. Somehow this gave her strength to endure the torment that

1

seethed inside her frozen form, and allowed her to contemplate the breath of movement behind her right shoulder without attempting to flee from it. Was it warm or was it cold? She struggled to describe it, as it was neither, yet it was both. Was it constant or was it intermittent? It was certainly constant. Why then did the flame move only occasionally? Surely this meant that the two phenomena were not linked. Yet she knew to the core of her being that they were. Why was there no sound? She could not divine the answer to that question.

The remains of the candle began to slide about in the pool of fat that had formed in its clay dish, and Molly knew that the guttering flame would soon be gone. Then she felt huge hands around her neck, crushing her throat, so that her scream was silenced before it began. She tried to stand, but the massive hands, while continuing to choke her, bore down on her and pinned her to the chair. She knew that she was fast losing consciousness, and could not hit out at the giant force that was destroying her.

Her body went limp in the aggressor's grasp. The hands shook her roughly as if to ascertain the truth of her collapse, before finally letting go of her. Then she fell to the floor, hitting her head hard on the flat uneven stones. The candle lost its tenuous connection with life. All was plunged into darkness, and the blood that flowed from Molly's head was invisible.

The entity faded from the room, leaving by the low door of the cottage, and melted away into the blackness of the winter's long night.

Samuel was looking forward to being back with Molly again. He and his two younger brothers, James and Alec, had done well, and were bringing home plenty of meat to share. Molly was an accomplished cook, and would put every morsel to good use, wasting nothing. Only another couple of miles, and they would be back with her, lighting up the fire, cracking jokes, and eating their fill. This image warmed him, and kept strength in his step as he led the way confidently along the dark track.

The three brothers had built the cottage together, finishing it two years ago. It was situated at a distance from the village of which it was a part, and was made of rough-hewn stones, many of which had come from a nearby ruin. A clear stream flowed close by, providing a supply of water that rarely failed. When daylight allowed, they were now working to complete an enclosure behind their dwelling, where they hoped to keep chickens, and grow some things to eat. At first, the cottage had consisted of only one room, where they cooked, lived and slept, but when Molly joined them, the brothers built another room on one end of it for Samuel and Molly to share at night. They sometimes joked about how they would build another room once several babies were born.

James and Alec liked Molly well enough. For one thing, her quiet competence in household matters reminded them of their mother, who had died long ago, trying to give birth to a baby who, had he survived, would have been their next brother. They had named him Nathaniel, and he was buried with their mother in the churchyard in the village. In his grief, their father had taken another wife, who had turned out to be the very opposite of their mother, and the brothers had planned to move out as soon as they were old enough to survive alone. Because they stuck together, that had turned out to be possible sooner than they had thought, and they had distanced themselves by choosing to build away from the village, the journey to their dwelling being more than half an hour on foot.

They had heard recently that there might be work for them all in the spring, summer and autumn. It was rumoured that the local landowner was looking for strong men with building skills, as he had plans afoot. No one knew exactly what he had in mind, but the brothers were keen to put themselves forward, eager to earn enough to buy a cow, and perhaps even a horse.

Molly was the daughter of a woman who used to keep house for the local doctor. Molly did not know who her father was, and no one else had offered any explanation for her appearance. All they knew was that one Monday morning, just over twenty years ago, the presence of Mrs Lark was first observed at the doctor's house, where she took over the housekeeping duties from the doctor's sister, who went away to be a companion to her ailing mother. The local people remarked upon the voluminous nature of Mrs Lark's skirts, until it became obvious that their bulk was not entirely due to the amount of material in them.

Sam remembered well his first sight of Molly. He was four years old, and she was a tiny baby. He had cut his hand badly on a rusty nail, and his mother had pleaded with the doctor to help. The doctor, being a kind man, had cleaned and dressed the wound for no fee. When Sam looked back, he knew that he had fallen in love with Molly then, and thereafter had waited patiently until he could ask her to marry him. He had waited until the day she turned sixteen. He had asked her, and she had said yes. The wedding had taken place two autumns ago, in the church next to where his mother and brother were buried. Molly had looked like an angel in the dress she had stitched for herself, and he was so proud to have her hand in his.

Sam quickened his step. They were now within minutes of the cottage. No light was visible. Molly must have put the blanket across the window already. Everything was still. The sky was overcast. There was barely any light from the stars, and the thin moon shone only weakly through the cloud. James and Alec were sauntering along, unconcerned about the time of their return. They had one another, and were caught up in an intense conversation about snares.

'Molly!' Sam called as he reached the cottage door. 'We are back!' He loosened his boots. Strange, he thought, she should be at the door by now.

He pushed the door open and stared into the total blackness. His chest tightened. Where was Molly? If she were here, she would be reaching out to him by the light of the single candle that should be burning on the table. He kicked his boots to one side, and moved forward. His foot connected with something solid, but which did not resist him entirely. A sleeping animal? Surely it could not be. Molly would not accommodate one here. Besides, there was no animal smell. He reached into his pocket for his tinderbox and the stub of candle that he always carried.

By the light of that candle he saw his dear Molly sprawled motionless on the floor, with a pool of blood by her head. Her face was devoid of colour, and her breathing was shallow and irregular. He knelt beside her, and for a moment he stroked the cold skin of her ashen face. He wanted to scream, but no sound came. He knew that James and Alec would be with them soon. They would not be able to take away the stark reality of this scene, but they would be with him.

Quickly he went to the bedroom, and brought the patchwork quilt that Molly had made for their bed. He wrapped her in it, and lit the fire that she had laid in the hearth. Whatever had happened to her must have been late in the day, as she always laid the fire just before dark. The flames crackled and spat. Then they leapt up and lit the room more clearly. He longed to lift her still body from the floor, but knew that this was not the best thing for her. He would wait until his brothers came. Then together they could put something under her to protect her from the cold of the stone floor.

He heard steps outside, and called, 'James! Alec! Come quick! A terrible thing has happened here today.'

His brothers burst in, not pausing to take off their boots. James saw Molly first, and he fell to his knees, caressing her hand and softly calling her name. Alec stood behind him, clutching his chest in agitation.

'We must get something beneath her,' said Sam urgently.

Without a word, Alec pulled his straw mattress to Molly's side, and together the three brothers gently moved her onto it. Then they moved the table to one side, and pulled her on the mattress into the centre of the room, in front of the fire.

James fetched water, and put the pot on the fire to boil. 'We must clean that wound,' he said tersely. 'I will tear my spare shirt into strips to bind it.'

Alec collected some of the precious salt from Molly's store, and searched for her box of the special moss that she kept clean and dry in case one of them sustained a deep cut. The brothers had been fascinated by the properties of that moss. They knew that Molly collected it from bogs, and she had showed them how the parts that lay against the stems made a natural wick that drew fluid and pus away from a wound.

It was then that Sam saw the state of Molly's neck. 'She has got mud on her neck,' he muttered. 'Where has that come from?' He reached out to stroke it away, and at that moment he realised these marks were not dirt at all. He grabbed the fresh candle that James had placed on the table, and he held it close to Molly's neck while he inspected the marks.

'These are finger marks!' he snarled angrily. He jumped to his feet. 'Who in heaven's name has done this? Whoever it is, I will kill him…'

James put his hand on Sam's shoulder. 'Steady, Sam,' he advised. 'Going after the invisible cannot make Molly well again. We must put all our strength into helping her.'

Sam's shoulders sagged. 'You are right, James,' he acknowledged.

Gradually they warmed Molly's frozen body. Alec and Sam carefully cleaned the gash on her head, covered it in the moss, and bound it with pieces of James' shirt. Alec took a small piece of the clean material, soaked it in boiled water, and used it to dampen her lips.

5

While they were doing this, James looked for timber so that he could make the door fast, and add extra barring to it. He had deterred Sam from searching for Molly's attacker, but his mind was full of violent hatred and revenge. Molly's state was truly pitiful to see, and he knew that she might not survive. If he could but find her assailant, he would kill him with his bare hands.

All the while, Molly lay limp and motionless. Sam scrutinised her face, trying to detect any flicker of an eyelid. He watched her hands, hoping to see even minute movement of a finger, but there was nothing. From time to time, he would raise her hand and forearm gently from the bed, but her muscles showed no response. He thought he could detect a shade of pink in her cheek, but on closer inspection he knew it had been but a trick of the light. The only change was that the ugly bruising on her neck became more pronounced.

At length, James offered to make some oat gruel for them all. He had no wish to cook any of the rabbit that they had caught, but knew that somehow each of them must take in nourishment. Silently, Sam and Alec acknowledged his offer, and he went about preparing their supper.

They ate little, and with no appetite, watching their beloved Molly, willing her to live. Alec toyed with the last spoonful in his bowl, and on impulse, dipped the knuckle of his little finger in it, and ran it along Molly's bottom lip. Although she did not move, he had the sense that she drew away from it in some indefinable way. As if guided, he stood up and went to the store alcove, and searched through its contents. His hand fell on the prized honey pot, and he raised the lid a fraction. There was but a smear left in the bottom of it. Carefully he ran his knuckle across it, as if to flavour it, and then returned to Molly's side.

He leaned towards Molly's ear and said, 'Molly, there is a sweet taste for you here, precious child.' He signalled to Sam to cradle her as best he could without disturbing her, and he wet the sweetened knuckle with his saliva. Then he ran it slowly along the path that the gruel had taken. Her lips parted, only by a fraction of an inch, but they definitely moved.

'Again, Alec, again,' Sam urged with desperation in his voice.

James put a hand on Sam's head and ruffled his hair. 'We must not rush it,' he murmured.

When Alec saw fit to repeat his action, the tip of Molly's tongue could be seen.

6

Sam leaned down and kissed her cheek slowly and gently, and he was rewarded by feeling her fingers twitch against the hand with which he caressed them.

Then, with hope of her survival in his heart, Sam turned to his brothers and said, 'A foul and evil deed was done this day to our dear Molly. I swear that I will find a way to avenge it.'

Each brother spat into a palm, and the three joined in what was now a pact between them. Each had his own thoughts of the identity of the monster, and each had plans for its tormented demise, but for now no one spoke them aloud. Their only words were kind and loving, so that Molly's hearing was not exposed to violent voices.

The three sat up late into the night, nursing the treasured woman who was to them a mother, their sister and Sam's wife. Such gentle attention could not have been improved upon. When at last sleep began to press them, they took it in turns to lie on James' mattress, so that there were always two who kept vigil – one to watch over Molly, and one to listen for any stirring outside.

Morning brought with it torrential rain.

'Curses,' muttered Sam darkly. 'I had planned to look for tracks, and now all signs will be washed away.' During the night, he had scrutinised every inch of their dwelling as best he could, but had found nothing unusual. His mind could not fathom how no disturbance to their home could be seen, despite the terrible damage that had been done to Molly.

He remained by her side, stroking her hair and speaking gently to her, reminding her of their life together. There had been times in the night when he had thought he had lost her, but there were times when she had stirred, and once, he fancied that she had whispered his name.

Wan daylight crept in through the small windows, and lit Molly's face as someone who was more alive than dead. The flutterings of hope that Sam had felt in his heart took a more definite form.

He turned to Alec. 'Broth,' he said decisively. 'The rabbit. Can you boil it and strain off the juices?'

Without a word, Alec went about his task, leaving Sam and James contemplating Molly's still frame.

'The danger to her life is not yet past, but her state looks something more like sleep now,' James observed.

'Aye,' Sam agreed, adding 'James, where can we get more honey?'

James shook his head. 'It is not plentiful hereabouts at the best of times, and at the end of the year...' His voice trailed off.

'Someone might have saved some for the feasting,' said Sam desperately.

'They might, but if they have they're not going to be giving any away.'

'Will you go and try to find some?' Sam pleaded.

'I will. I'll do anything for our Molly. But I fear I shall come back empty-handed.'

The doctor and Molly's mother had died some years before, and no one had come to replace them. The brothers knew that they had to rely entirely on their own skills and instincts. Molly herself was adept at nursing, having seen so much during her upbringing, but she was in no state to nurse herself.

'I will ask at the stables,' James decided. He put on his boots, flung his thick woollen cape across his shoulders, and was gone.

While Alec prepared the broth, Sam made a minute study of the marks on Molly's neck, until their pattern was embedded in his memory. One thing that became clear to him was that the hands that had caused this damage were enormous. What creature possessed such hands? He stared at his own strong hands. They were bigger than most, and yet they were not anywhere near the size of those that had so sorely damaged his beloved Molly. He became aware that as well as caring for Molly, they would have to be watchful for their own safety. The beast could be lurking nearby, and it might strike again. He knew instinctively that it would not hold back from attacking any of them.

When the clear brown liquid was ready, Alec and Sam worked together to transfer it, drip by drip, so that Molly's unresisting mouth could absorb it without danger of choking. Thus the feeding of the contents of a small horn spoon took an eternity. But Alec and Sam were oblivious of the passage of time. All they cared about was keeping Molly alive.

Nightfall came again. Alec lit a candle, and stirred up the fire.

'I shall spend the daylight hours tomorrow bringing in more fuel,' he told Sam. 'We are going to need a lot more than we had bargained for this winter.'

There was no sign of James that evening, or indeed that night, but the next morning brought him back. Alec and Sam had taken it in turns to

moaned. He was inconsolable.

Alec sat with Molly, patiently resuming the task of tending her motionless lips with the cloth wetted from the cup of boiled water.

Sam tore away from James, and went outside. His brothers made no move to follow him. He did not go far, and they could hear him sobbing. He later returned, silent but much calmer, to take up his position by his wife.

An hour or so passed, and Molly's breathing became normal, with colour returning to her cheeks. When Sam saw this, he sighed, and then went about making a kind of support for her back, ready for when she might try to sit again. This proved to be time well spent, because by midday she was conscious, and she indicated that she would like to drink.

This time, Alec and James sat either side of her, and Sam took her hands from the front. Together they raised her to a half-sitting position, with the support pulled in behind her. This worked well, and she lay there, weary, but relaxed and comfortable. James steadied her head, while Alec carefully fed the water into her mouth, allowing her time to swallow.

She managed this well, and Alec asked if she would like some oat gruel, an offer which she accepted in the same silent way. Alec was cautious, giving her only a small amount, and when she searched for more, he said, 'Soon.' Despite Sam's insistence, he would not be swayed from this decision, stating that little and often was the need of the sick.

Each day saw progress in Molly's condition, and by the end of a week, she was sitting in a chair for most of the day, taking some interest in whatever was happening around her. The only thing that did not change was her speech. She had none. She could say no words, and she could not even make a sound. The brothers made no attempt to coax her, believing that it was too soon for such action. Still she slept in the main room, with the fire glowing through the night, and one of them always watching over her.

The gash on her head was healing well with the aid of the special moss, and she was left with a scar that would recede. Her physical beauty had not been unduly marred, but her voice had been stolen, and it seemed that a part of her personality had been shattered. The slightest sound, familiar or unusual, would leave her nervous and edgy, and the brothers took to speaking aloud about their actions and their thoughts in an attempt to limit the impact of their movements upon her. They took especial care not to approach her from behind, or indeed to pass near her back, as such movement would invariably provoke alarm in her.

Sometimes the distant clattering of dead leaves blown against the door would startle them all. Awake or sleeping, the brothers were constantly aware of unnamed danger, and they grew used to avoiding any depth of slumber. When working outside, they would talk to each other in low tones about their fears of the return of the monster. Had it been a monster, or was it a man with monstrous hands? Why had it come? How had it known to come? Their cottage was off the beaten track, and it was rare that anyone passed. Would the creature return, and if so, when? There were ever more questions, and no answers. All they could do was to plan their defences to be impregnable – guarding Molly at all times within, and outside keeping careful watch, whenever possible moving only as a pair.

Midwinter came and went. The bitter wind howled. It screamed and raged past the cottage, unable to batter its way inside, and it moaned eerily as it eddied past the half-built walls of the enclosure. At this time of year, they blocked the windows with animal skins day and night, to preserve every fragment of warmth that the fire gave out. Snow piled up against the door, deadening the few sounds that might have come from outside. The brothers spent much time keeping a way open to the track to the village, in case it were needed.

Before the onset of the snow, they had carried more fuel from the cave, and stacked it inside the cottage. By great good fortune, on their last trip to the cave, Alec and James had come across a newly-dead deer – old and tough, but nothing that a good boiling would not put right. Being a generous and fair man, the landowner had long let it be known that although hunters would be shown no mercy, deer that died naturally could be claimed by the local people. The brothers had jammed pieces of it in the rocks high up at the back of the cave, and had carried the rest home, hanging it on the outer wall of the bedroom, which now served as a store.

As time passed, the brothers did all they could to devise ways of helping Molly to speak again. She showed some pleasure at some of their attempts, and would sometimes even try to mouth words in response to their encouragement, but still she uttered no sound.

Week by week, they created a simple language of signs and gestures that she could make to alert them first to her needs, and later to simple ideas and thoughts. There was plenty of time for them to practise this new art together, and for certain easy interactions, it became more than adequate.

Whatever they were doing, the brothers made certain that Molly was never left alone in that room – not even for a moment – and they noticed that with the passage of time, her face slowly began to lose the shocked, hunted look that had pervaded it for so long.

Alec would sometimes sit with her while carving pieces of hardwood into useful shapes. She would watch this activity intently, and one day he began to teach her this craft. As the winter progressed, she became quite skilled – carving models of small animals and birds. James made a box for her to keep them in, and she kept it in the centre of the table where the candle had stood on that fateful night.

Eventually they took Molly for short walks outside, and she showed pleasure at the sight of such simple things as the frost-rimmed stalks of grass and the icicles hanging from the banks of the stream. Yet still she did not speak.

Chapter Two

Spring was a long time in coming, but in March, when things began to stir, the brothers heard that the landowner had plans to build a new store and also a number of dwellings for the workers that he needed. He had decided that he would no longer depend on itinerant labour, and would create a permanent workforce upon which he could call in any eventuality.

It became very clear that he was keen to obtain the services of men such as Sam, Alec and James for the next year or two, and possibly three, because they were known as competent builders. He sent the farrier to let them know that he wanted to see them.

After the farrier had delivered his message, the brothers sat down for a talk.

'We cannot leave Molly on her own,' said Sam flatly.

Alec and James looked at him, startled.

'We had no idea like that in our heads,' they pronounced together.

'We will work in rotation,' James suggested. 'The days will soon be long. Between the three of us, there can be a start at dawn, and a finish at nightfall.'

Molly was listening intently. She became agitated, and Sam held her, intending to soothe her. But she wriggled out of his arms and went to the fire, where she pulled ash out and spread it out to cool. Then she began to draw something in the ash.

'A picture!' said James. 'Look, Sam. Look what she is doing.'

Sam was ecstatic. Apart from the carving that Alec had taught her to do, this was the first thing she had tried to create since he had found her near death. All these months, she had done no sewing, knitting, cooking or cleaning. Instead she had spent many of her hours staring into space.

'A picture of great complexity,' he said proudly as he watched her.

She turned to him, shook her head in what appeared to be exasperation, and continued her task.

When she had finished, she pulled the brothers close to it, and guided them by pointing to each part in a certain sequence.

Sam strained to understand, but felt defeated.

'Molly, I cannot work out what you mean,' he admitted.

Molly repeated her actions, but Sam felt just as blank as before.

'I think 'tis a kind of map,' said James suddenly.

Molly nodded vigorously. Once more she went through her actions.

'I am beginning to see it,' Alec announced excitedly. 'Molly is trying to show us something about plans for work.'

Molly patted his shoulder, and drew him closer to her ash drawing, demonstrating over and over again what she was trying to communicate.

At last, Alec said, 'I see it now. It shows us an idea of how to work without leaving her, and without losing many hours travelling back and forth. She is saying that some of the time she will come with us and help.'

'She cannot,' stated Sam adamantly.

'Why not?' asked Alec. 'She wants to try.'

Sam looked very worried. ''Tis not women's work, and we will not be able to watch her closely enough.'

James looked thoughtful. 'We could speak to the farrier's wife,' he suggested slowly.

Sam looked unconvinced, but Molly tried to drag him nearer to her drawing, beckoning to James and Alec to help her. Then she added a square where the farrier's house stood, on the way to the landlord's dwelling. In the end Sam agreed with reluctance to speak to the farrier's wife. In itself that would not be a difficult task, as she had been almost the first to hear of their misfortune. The difficulty would be in devising a plan for Molly's safety – a plan that he could trust completely.

When the day came for them to meet the landowner, they all set off at dawn together. The farrier's wife, whose name was Betty, was more than willing for Alec and Molly to sit with her, while James and Sam, the strong-looking ones, went to speak to the landowner. Molly and Betty clearly liked each other well enough, and Betty showed Molly some new stitches as they waited for the others to return. Alec concealed his delight about this, as he did not want anything to disturb Molly's new-found interest.

It was several hours later that Sam and James returned, almost jubilant.

Sam began to tell the others what had taken place. 'The landowner knew of our plight, and he would not countenance any situation where Molly was left alone. He wants our labour, and asks that we work all the hours we can, while keeping her safe. He will provide food for us as we work, and will pay us for our labour in grain, seeds, roots and maybe even stock.'

James continued. 'We start next month, so we will have to get on and finish the work behind our cottage by then.'

Betty coughed a little into her handkerchief, and the men turned to her. 'I am glad of your news,' she told them. 'For my part, I am growing more advanced in years. My daughter, although still young, has left home to marry a churchman, and lives a day's ride away. I see her barely once a month, and I am weary at times without company. My husband needs me to cook his meals, but I would welcome another woman in the house. Molly and I are comfortable together.' Here she turned to Molly. 'Are we not, my dear?'

Molly looked relaxed and happy, and nodded her head.

Betty went on. 'Sam, can your wife come here for three days of each week?'

Sam could see that Molly looked radiant.

'Molly's face is the only answer we need,' he replied. 'We will come on the first day of April, or sooner if your master sends for us.'

That night, Sam took Molly to their room for the first time since their lives had been changed. She went with him eagerly, and they slept curled up together, next to the last of the winter store of grain.

Chapter Three

The brothers worked hard to complete their enclosure as soon as possible. It was a good size, extending back a considerable way, and much wider than the cottage itself. Once it was secure, they began to prepare the ground for seeding.

But then word came that the Master was in need of them straight away. Fire had broken out in an upper room of his extensive dwelling, and although the flames had been extinguished and no one had been hurt, some roof timbers had been badly affected, and their charred remains might collapse at any time. That night the brothers gathered their tools and made everything ready for the next day, when they would leave early for work.

Molly and Sam had continued to sleep together. That night Molly was restless, and Sam was often disturbed. Although he grumbled quietly to himself, he was pleased, since it was clear that she was excited by the prospect of what the next day would bring.

The following morning they were all ready in good time, and they set off across the open moor at the crack of dawn. The air was crisp, and their breath showed as clouds of mist. This route was by far the quickest way to make their journey, as following the track meant going to the village, and from there heading towards their destination, thus adding miles to their journey. Except in broad daylight, crossing the moor could be hazardous, but daylight hours were now extending. There would be plenty of time for a full day's work before they were forced to retrace their steps in advance of darkness.

Molly waved goodbye to the brothers as Betty opened her door, pleasure showing clearly on her face, and she disappeared into the house without a backward glance. Sam was much reassured to observe this. Throughout the journey he had rehearsed in his mind the possibility that she would take fright at the last moment, but now he could see that his fears had been entirely unfounded. He continued on with a spring in his step, his brothers following close behind him.

Inside Betty's home, Molly was invited to take a cup of nettle tea before beginning the day's activities.

'My mother was a seamstress,' Betty explained. 'She was always in great demand. Any woman who could afford to employ her would do so without hesitation, knowing that the work would be sound, and would last.'

Molly nodded, and Betty continued.

'She taught me a great deal. I have never been as gifted, but I am better than most. Sadly, my daughter has not the patience for it. Of course, I insisted that she learned everything she needed to know, but beyond that I could not persuade her. She is an excellent cook though, and very thrifty,' she added proudly. Here she paused, and finished off her tea before adding conspiratorially, 'I would be happy to teach you all I know. Then you will be able to earn a tidy sum for yourself, as well as keeping house. What do you think?'

Molly was clearly excited by this proposition. She nodded her head vigorously, and looked around the room to see if Betty had laid anything out for her attention. She saw nothing, so returned her gaze to Betty and waited.

Betty stood up. 'Fetch that low chair, and follow me,' she instructed.

Obediently Molly picked up the chair on which she had been sitting. Betty led the way to a small room that was immediately behind the one they had left. Molly placed the chair where Betty directed, and then Betty began to pull various materials and threads out of a wooden chest, and spread them out.

Molly feasted her eyes on the bright colours, and Betty had to speak to her twice before she realised that she was being encouraged to sit down and start her work.

The morning flew past, and Betty left Molly so that she could prepare food for her husband. Once he was fed and back to work, she and Molly ate bread and soup together before continuing with their labours. Sometimes they worked in silence, apart from Betty giving instructions, but at other times Betty would tell stories from her life, in which Molly demonstrated much interest through smiles, nods and other gestures.

The brothers came for Molly before sunset, allowing sufficient time for most of their journey home to be complete by full darkness. Their mood was cheerful as they strode along. Their work had barely tired them. Alec and James broke into song, and Sam joined in with the chorus as he walked by Molly's side, holding her hand tightly. Once, he fancied he could hear her humming, but then he realised that it was the sound of an underground stream coursing nearby.

True to his word, their employer had seen to it that they were nourished during the day, and they had been fed very well. This left them with a little time on their hands during the evening, and they played a game that they had invented two winters before. It was made out of numerous small sticks, and the rules were quite complicated.

They were up early again the following morning, and they set out eagerly in the clear air, moving swiftly, and saying little. The sky showed promise of a fine day, and the brothers looked forward greatly to continuing their work on the damaged roof in preparation for its repair. Molly's mind was filled with patterns of complex stitching that she had already learned, and was hungry for more.

They found Betty at her door, looking out for them. She waved to them from a distance, thus showing that her eyesight was good for her age. Then she stood there, waiting.

Betty had already found Molly to be an apt and eager pupil, and she had woken that morning with a sense of purpose that she had not felt since her daughter, Jane, had left home. Apart from the daily bustle of preparing meals, and seeing to the washing and cleaning, the house had seemed devoid of life. Her husband made no sign of being aware of this, and this increased her sense of emptiness. The addition of Molly in her life was like moving from night to day. Secretly she had already entertained the idea of asking her to come for more of the weekdays, and perhaps even to sleep a night or more. She could make a space in their small workroom, and put down a straw mattress. However, she was aware that such invitations, if made too hastily, may not be of benefit to the inviter or the invited. She decided to say nothing meanwhile, but to consider future possibilities.

Molly left the others, and ran the last part with the air of someone who felt a lightness inside her. She unlatched the gate, and sped up the path without a backward glance. Together, she and Betty disappeared into the house, and were soon hard at work.

After the third day, it was all Betty could do to keep herself from pressing Molly to come the next morning, but she held her impulse to herself, and said she would see her the following week, as agreed.

That evening, there was a scene at the cottage that was very close to an argument between Sam and Molly. Sam began to talk to Alec and James about who would stay at home with Molly the next day, but Molly was having none of this, and stood in front of Sam, shaking her head vehemently. At first, Sam took this good-naturedly, leaning to one side of her and then the other, in an attempt to continue his conversation with his brothers. But when she put both her hands firmly to his mouth, he lost patience.

He stood up and wagged his finger in her face, saying, 'Molly, you will do what we decide.'

Molly looked extremely angry, and for a moment it looked as if she were about to slap him, but then, to everyone's concern, she collapsed into a chair, and began crying, her body racked with silent sobs.

Instantly, Sam looked shame-faced, and became calm. He put an arm round her and said, 'Molly, one of us has got to stay here with you. We were just deciding who that would be for tomorrow.'

She did not respond, except in that she did not push him away.

When she stopped crying, she stood up, again spread out the ash and began to draw.

It was Alec who recognised first what she was depicting.

'Here's our cottage with the four of us in it. Here we are walking together across the moor, past Betty's house and on from there. Ah! There are still four of us. Sam, Molly wants to come to work with us.'

'That cannot be,' stated Sam firmly. ''Tis no place for women. She cannot work on that dangerous building with us.'

Molly brushed the picture out of the ashes and began again. This time she drew herself, sitting on a rock, watching the others work.

'But what would you do there, all day?' asked Sam incredulously. 'No, it just would not work.'

Molly took hold of his arms, trying to shake him.

'All right, all right,' said Sam. 'We will think of something else.'

He stood up and paced around the room for a while. Then he slipped on his boots and stepped out into the night. He did not go far. He stood a little way from the front of the cottage, and took several deep breaths. He felt agitated by what had taken place, and he could not think of a solution to his dilemma. Molly could not sit on a rock all day, she could not work with them, and she could not stay here at the cottage alone. He could see no other options.

Then a thought struck him. Perhaps she would be willing to compromise. She could walk with them to work, watch until they stopped to eat, and then one of them would walk back with her. He returned to put this to her.

After Sam had presented his plan, Molly appeared perplexed. She

22

avoided his eyes, and then hung her head for a while. But when she looked up, it was clear that her mind was made up, and she smiled at them all, nodding. Then she picked three sticks from their winter game, one slightly longer than the others, hid them behind her back, and then presented them as if they were equal. The brothers took one each. It was Alec who had the long one, and so it would be he who would come home with Molly the next day.

'We could do some work in the enclosure,' he said cheerfully. 'The soil is drying up a little now, and 'tis a good time to dig.'

Sam looked uncomfortable. 'Do not take your eyes off Molly.'

Alec looked grim. 'Sam, I will guard her with my life.'

Chapter Four

And so the days passed until it was time for Molly to return to see Betty. There was an extra spring in her step as she set off, slightly ahead of the others. She waved excitedly when she saw Betty waiting at the door, and when she came to the gate, she ran lightly down the path, as if she had no cares in the world. Sam smiled at his brothers, and they hurried on, to begin work.

As Betty and Molly sat in the workroom, busy with their stitching, Betty told stories of her childhood, and tales that her mother had handed down to her. Molly made many signs that showed her intense interest, and Betty's only sadness was that they had no way of sharing their thoughts more directly.

By the end of April, the brothers had earned enough seeds to sow in their enclosure, and had been promised chickens very soon. This meant that whoever was with Molly on her cottage days worked hard to finish the final preparation of their piece of land. Their secret objective was to have earned a bulling heifer by the autumn – a beast that they would tether near the cottage on ground that was for common use.

On the first day of May, Molly jumped out of bed, full of expectation of the pleasures of a day with Betty, but then she clutched herself and ran outside. Sam followed her speedily, and found her sitting on a rock, her face very pale.

'What is it?' he asked worriedly.

Molly shook her head, pushed him away, and went back in the house. But he noticed that she ate no porridge, and that her pale face did not regain its former colour. He kept a close eye on her as they crossed the moor. She walked at her usual speed, but she certainly did not look sprightly this morning. And he observed Betty giving her a penetrating look as she ushered her quickly into her home and shut the door firmly behind her.

Once the two women were seated, Betty said, 'You are looking a little pale this morning.' She paused, and then added meaningfully,

'You might have a chill coming on.'

Molly kept her gaze fastened upon her work, and shook her head.

Betty did not press her. Instead she plied her with cups of calming herb infusions. She decided that she would question her further the next day.

The next morning was much the same. Molly again ran out of the cottage, and Sam followed her to find her on the same rock, looking paler than she had the day before.

'I think you should stay here today,' he decided. 'I will be here with you.'

She shook her head carefully, and made her way back into the cottage to get dressed. The brothers had to slow their pace across the moor that morning.

She was hardly seated in Betty's workroom, when Betty said, 'Molly, I think you are with child.'

Molly froze, and a tear escaped from the corner of her left eye. As she hurried to conceal it, she changed her mind, and threw herself into Betty's arms.

'There, there, dear,' Betty soothed. 'It comes to us all, sooner or later, except for the poor few who are barren. This is a time when a woman needs her mother, and I am sorry that yours passed away so early in her life. You will have to make do with me instead.'

Molly drew away, and stared at Betty incredulously. She opened her mouth spontaneously, and a very small sound came from somewhere at the back of her throat. Then she clutched desperately at her neck and looked terrified, as if she were being hunted for her life.

Betty pulled Molly's hands from her throat, and held them together between her own, rubbing them gently.

'Now, now,' she murmured, 'there's no harm will come to you here.'

Then her voice took on a brisk tone. 'We have plenty to get ready before you give birth. We will finish stitching these shirts for the Master. With your help I am well ahead with his present order, and we will soon turn our hands to making clothes ready for the little one.' Molly began to relax a little, and Betty continued. 'And I am going to tell that husband of yours that you must come here every day from now on – except Sundays of course.'

Molly felt very strange. She took her head in her hands, and slowly moved it a little from side to side, and then up and down, as if discovering that it belonged to her. Yes, that was the feeling. Yet her head must always have been a part of her. She felt very disorientated. Nothing seemed to make sense. She swayed a little, and feeling inexplicably exhausted, she closed her eyes.

'What is it dear?' asked Betty, her concern making her forget for a moment that Molly could not reply.

Molly could hear Betty's voice as if from far away, through a very thick fog. Her words seemed foreign. She opened her eyes again, but could not focus them, and Betty's form seemed to swirl and then break into tiny pieces. Trying to steady herself, she clutched at the back of her chair, but this served only to increase her confusion.

'I will fetch you a cup of my best camomile tea,' Betty decided. She stood up stiffly, and left the room, leaving the door wide open.

Molly stared after her. Distress and panic threatened to overwhelm her, but then she heard clattering sounds coming from the kitchen that were unmistakeable in their quality, and she knew that they signified safety. She wondered if she should follow Betty, but decided against it for now. Her legs felt strangely weak, and she did not want to cause any further disturbance by stumbling.

Molly sat down, picked up her needlework, and was about to continue where she had left off, when she began to realise that she had done no stitching at home in the cottage for a long time. How strange. Why was that? she wondered. Her work fell into her lap as she contemplated what seemed to be an insoluble question.

Then her thoughts were interrupted by Betty returning with the promised cup of tea.

'Here you are, dear,' said Betty. 'Sip it slowly. It will do you the world of good. 'Tis made from the best camomile. I gathered it myself last summer.'

Glad to follow Betty's simple instruction, she sampled the drink, and soon felt further calmed by it.

When later the brothers came to collect Molly, Betty waved her off, but made an excuse to detain Alec, feigning a need for some heavy object to be shifted in advance of her husband's return.

She took him round the back of the house, and as soon as she was certain of being out of earshot, she told him what had happened, making him promise to tell Sam as soon as he could. Realising immediately the importance of what he had learned, Alec agreed and sped off, joining the others only minutes later.

'What was it?' asked Sam good-naturedly.

Alec caught his eye as Molly bent to collect a feather. He put a finger to his lips, and made it plain that there was something urgent to tell. From her crouched position, Molly sensed that covert communication had taken place, but she chose to behave as if she were unaware of it. Instead, she stuck the feather at a jaunty angle in her plaited black hair, and continued on her way.

At home, she insisted on being the one to start the fire, pushing away any help. Although the days were opening out and the sun could be quite warm, the evenings still brought with them the kind of chill that needed the flames from burning logs. James began making their simple meal, and Sam and Alec went outside. Molly could hear them talking in low voices, but she could not make out what they were saying. She went to the bedroom, and fetched some scraps of material from her meagre collection. Then she sat at the fire, and threaded a needle.

James noticed straight away what she was doing, but made no comment, thinking it best to behave as if nothing unusual was happening. He knew only too well that although she stitched every day that she was in Betty's company, she had not touched her sewing here since that fateful day last December. Molly was grateful for his silence, as she wanted to focus her mind on the questions that had come into it that afternoon.

She was aware of the return of Sam and Alec, but they too made no comment, and instead spoke between themselves. The sound of their voices receded as she thought of the afternoon with Betty that had just passed. With child…? I am with child? What joyous news! Fleetingly she brushed her hand over her belly, before continuing with her stitching. She wished fervently that her mother and the doctor were still alive. They would have been so glad for her. But instead she was surrounded by others who would be happy. Betty had already pledged to help her to prepare. Her heart leaped at the thought of creating tiny clothes, neatly fashioned. She must ask the others to collect long twigs from the willow trees, so that she could weave a basket for the baby to sleep in, and she would dry plenty of her special moss for the baby to lie on. But why had she not stitched here, by her own fire, for so many months? She sighed, silently, and laid her work down for a moment. Then her hands strayed to her neck. Why was this? She felt disturbed, but then remembered Betty's motherly presence, and the cup of soothing tea. She wished she could ask the men to answer her question, but that was impossible. She could not speak, and she could not think of any way to depict her request. But why could she not speak? She had spoken for most of her life. Why was it that the power of speech was denied to her? More questions... and no answers. She remembered speaking last spring, she remembered it in the summer, and she remembered singing as she sat and sewed in the autumn. So where had her voice gone, and when did it go? She touched her throat again.

Although Sam had been sitting at the table talking to James and Alec, he had been watching Molly out of the corner of his eye. When he saw her touch her throat a second time, he stood up and went to her side. He wanted to talk to her about her child, their child, but he did not know how to begin, and most of all he wanted to wait until they were in the privacy of their own room. So he stroked her neck where the terrible marks had been, in a mistaken attempt to smooth away any memory of them that might have lingered in corners of her mind. He and his brothers had always taken great care never to mention the horrors of the attack that had been made upon her.

Yet in truth, these efforts had been futile, and the effect on Molly of what had been done to her had remained locked deep inside her. As the visible effects had dwindled and faded, the brothers had wrongly believed that Molly's memories had disappeared with them. Yet Betty's motherly approach about her pregnancy had almost breached the walls inside her that had entombed this knowledge.

Molly determinedly resolved to devise a way of eliciting answers to the questions that crowded her mind. Drawing away from her husband, she leaned to spread ash once more. At one side she depicted herself on a chair, sewing. Moving to the other side, she drew herself sitting, her hands not employed. Returning to the first drawing, she traced alongside it the shape of a head with its mouth open, and by the second drawing, the head she created had its mouth shut. Then she passed a twig to Sam and pointed to the space in the middle.

Sam took the twig reluctantly. He hung his head. He fiddled with one end of the twig, and made no move to follow Molly's direction. Undeterred, Molly took another, and handed it to James, who unsuccessfully tried to turn from her gaze. He too did nothing. Exasperated, she thrust a third stick into Alec's hands.

Alec turned to Sam and said, 'There is no doubt what Molly is asking. Who will tell her?'

Sam jumped up and began to shout. For a moment Molly

cowered in her seat, and he instantly fell silent and sat down again. But it was clear that she was not going to give up. She kept looking at each of the brothers in turn, pointing insistently at the space in the ash.

Seeing no way out of his dilemma, Sam began to speak to her.

'Molly, it was early in December. We three had been away, snaring rabbits. We had left before daylight, and were returning after dark, bearing what we had caught. I looked for the light at the window, but saw nothing, and thought you had covered it to keep out the cold. When I came in, I found you on the floor in the dark, left for dead.' He took her hand and put a finger of it to her head where the wound had healed. 'There was a great gash here, and a lot of your blood. We nursed you, and by great mercy, you lived, but you could not speak, and you did none of the household things you had done before.'

Molly had been listening intently, her eyes never straying from Sam's face. Now, she pointed to her neck, again and again.

At this moment, Sam's voice failed him, and he turned to James, who continued the story.

'Bruises began to show on your neck – bruises that had come from the grip of hands so huge that Sam's hands could not span the marks.'

Molly's face had been growing pale, but her energies did not leave her. She was very accustomed to Sam's unusually big hands, and she found it hard to imagine the size of those that had attacked her. Instinctively, she turned in her chair to look behind her, but could see only the rough, blank cottage wall.

'Aye,' James confirmed, 'whatever it was must have come from behind you.'

Although deeply shocked by these revelations, at the same time Molly felt a strange sense of relief. It was as if she had known all of this before.

Now Alec started to speak. 'We have watched over you night and day ever since, and we have been alert to any unknown danger to ourselves, but we have seen nothing. Torrential rain on the night we found you washed away any possible signs outside, there was nothing inside the cottage, and we have encountered no one who has seen such a beast. To this day we have no more clues about the identity of the attacker.'

Whereas before, Molly had come to experience the brothers' attentions as stifling, now she knew the reason for their vigilance, she felt deeply grateful for their devotion. She stood up, kissed each one in turn, and then went to the bedroom, where she made herself ready for the night.

Sam, James and Alec spent the next few minutes together, swearing allegiance to their pact – the agreement that they had made to discover the monster, and destroy it.

Then Sam left the others and joined Molly in their bed. He held her tight and said, 'You are carrying our child now. By the end of the year we will have a son or a daughter. If it is a son, he should look like me, and if it is a daughter, she must look like you.'

Molly smiled at Sam in the dark, and although he could not see it, he felt the warmth of it.

imagined. She had never seen the sea, but she had heard plenty about it from those who had. It sounded exciting and wondrous, but she was also glad that she had no need to approach it in all its swirling vastness.

Perhaps this cloth had been brought across the sea from one of those distant places? Fleetingly she wished that she could own a little of it herself – a small piece to sew into the patchwork coverings for her baby's basket – but she knew that taking even a few inches of it would cost her her job. She would never be trusted again, by the Master, or by anyone else who learned of her dishonesty.

Molly leaned back against the wall behind her, and closed her eyes to rest them for a moment. Black thread against black material could be a trial to her vision, even in sunlight. The intense sunlight of today warmed her body, but was a little harsh for staring at the cloth, and she gestured to Betty, indicating a request go indoors for a while.

'That was in my own mind,' was Betty's immediate response, and they went indoors to the small workroom.

The butterfly continued its movements. Its flutterings came in occasional bursts, and Molly wondered if a chrysalis had been growing inside her from which the baby was now trying to emerge, but was resting, exhausted, between attempts. Anxious, she wondered if it might fly away from her, but reassured herself that this could not be. She had certainly never heard of such a thing, and if it had been possible, she should surely have heard it spoken of in the doctor's house.

Molly felt no more movement inside her as she crossed the moor that evening with Sam, James and Alec, and she became worried. What had happened to the little one? But in bed that night, she felt it again. Smiling in the darkness, she took Sam's hand and placed it where he too could feel it. But the movements of their child were imperceptible to him.

Sam was heartened by Molly's action. He could tell that her belly was larger than he had known it before, and he had certain knowledge that this was not just from good feeding. He liked the way she had shared this with him. Yet he did not know what else she was experiencing, because she could not tell him.

The routine of the past weeks had left Sam more confident about Molly's safety and their future together. The hard work through the days strengthened his body and his mind, and he and his brothers talked of their plans for their enclosure, and for the family that they would rear together. Neither James nor Alec had made any mention of finding wives for themselves, and their spoken plans always portrayed the four of them as a unit, with Sam and Molly's offspring as close to them as children of their own would be. Sam had ceased to question this. His brothers' devotion to Molly's safety and wellbeing was absolute, and their plans were a natural consequence of this.

The next day Molly woke very early, when the brothers were still sound asleep. Slowly, carefully, and with infinite patience, she slipped out of bed, creating no movement that could prompt Sam into wakefulness. She crept noiselessly past the blanket that screened their room from the cottage, and then made her way round the sleeping forms of James and Alec, and reached the door. Inch by inch, she eased it open, fearful of its making a creak that would waken those who guarded her. Three months had passed since the brothers had ceased their nightly vigils, and with the passage of time they had grown used to entering the deeper layers of slumber again. They did not stir. She slipped through the small opening that she had created, and drew the door shut behind her, thus ensuring that there was no draught to alert James and Alec of her absence.

She stood outside and breathed deeply. Freedom! The sky was slowly filling with light, showing her the changing patterns of the clouds. Excited, she loosened her jet-black hair from its tightly-bound plait, and tossed it around her shoulders. Then she walked quickly and silently away from the cottage, before running back and to in the vibrant long grasses that flanked the path to the stream, where she crouched and took a long drink. Although they had had little rain for many weeks, the water was still clear and swift-running, and she savoured it. She still remembered the taste of the water at the doctor's house, and it compared very unfavourably with this purity, as did the taste from the skin bucket that they used to carry water to the cottage for the cooking. She washed her face, and then went in search of flowers, which she planned to fashion into a garland for her head. She moved from plant to plant, often spying another flower at a distance that promised to suit her purpose.

Satisfied that she had sufficient blooms in her hand, she made the garland, singing an occasional note to the small birds that twittered their songs and darted about in search of insects. Both she and the birds were unaware of the momentous import of her contribution to their music.

my life. It was when I was a child. There was an old woman in the village where I lived who could make such decoration. She would sit all day with bobbins in her hands, flicking them one way and then another. I used to like to sit beside her and watch, but I never learned how to do it.' Her voice took on a note of regret. 'I wish that I had.' She sighed. 'I have seen much decoration for dresses since, but never the like of what that woman made until I opened this pouch.'

Molly felt an overwhelmingly passionate desire to be able to create something as beautiful as this lace. She felt it as a craving in her soul, and at that moment she promised herself that one day she would find a way. For now she must content herself with learning all she could from Betty. Since she had been coming here, she had already absorbed many of her skills, and she knew there was much more that she could learn. Betty was a willing teacher, and Molly was an eager pupil.

Betty carefully returned the lace to its velvet pouch.

'We will stitch this in place once the garments are well-nigh complete,' she announced. She continued excitedly. 'Molly, I can hardly wait. Soon we will meet Mistress Mary. We shall impress her, and after that we shall not want for work.'

That night, Molly lay awake, her head too full of all the new things that were crowding into their lives. The baby that Sam had put inside her was growing, she was going to become an accomplished seamstress, she and Betty would soon see Mistress Mary for a fitting, and the brothers were gaining such favour with the Master that day by day their future prospects were greatly enhanced. And she wanted to find a way of learning how to make lace... Sam was sleeping quietly, but she could hear the comforting sound of gentle snoring coming from James or Alec. Then she stroked her belly until she fell asleep.

Chapter Seven

It was not long before Betty learned that she and Molly were to see
Mistress Mary at the Master's house. On the appointed day a servant
would be sent to carry everything that they required. Although Betty
grumbled about the pain in her knees preventing her from walking that
far, her voice carried an air of anticipation and excitement.

''Tis many a long year since I was inside that house,' she
confided. 'It must have been when the Master's father died and his
mother came to stay for a while. She already had her clothes for
mourning, but she wanted two nightdresses. I was summoned to take
measurements.' She lowered her voice, and Molly leaned her head
towards her. 'Between you and me, she was a harsh woman with a
sharp tongue, and I was not unhappy when I did not have to see her
again. My husband delivered the nightdresses, and the Master gave
him payment. I heard nothing more. Molly, 'tis my guess that the
Master and his sister have had a burden lifted from them by the death
of their mother. Now, when we go to the Master's house, mind you
tie your hair back well, and wear a fresh apron.'

Molly had already made plans to do exactly this, and she nodded
her head vigorously to assure Betty that there would be no cause for
concern about her appearance.

When the day arrived, Molly appeared at Betty's house looking very
neat. Betty threw up her hands in delight.

'Mercy me!' she exclaimed. 'I could not have wanted for better.'
Then she caught sight of Molly's fingernails, and took one of her
hands in order to examine the nails more closely. 'Well, bless you,
Molly!' she declared. 'What a pretty sight! And how did you get
them to look so smooth and clean?'

Molly smiled. She rubbed her hands together vigorously, as if
washing them, and then she went outside for a moment, and returned
carrying a smooth stone. Then she set about showing Betty how she
had achieved the admired result.

'You are a clever one!' exclaimed Betty delightedly.

Betty herself was wearing a dress that Molly had not seen before, and when she noted Molly's interest, she rustled her skirt and confided proudly, "'Tis my Sunday dress. An' I have rubbed my knees with goose fat, so they should carry me up to the house.' She beamed at Molly with satisfaction. 'Now we are to get everything ready for the servant.'

Together they wrapped the two dresses carefully in old sheets that Betty kept especially for such a purpose, and they secured these large parcels by tying the corners of the sheets together, and binding them with strips of old cloth, joined to make a good length. In a patchwork bag, Betty packed pins, needles and thread. Her hand hovered over the lace, but she decided against bringing it, lest by some misfortune it were mislaid.

The servant arrived in the late morning. Molly was puzzled by this, as their services were not required until the afternoon, and the journey to the Master's house would not take long, even at Betty's slow pace. However, she soon learned from Betty that it was customary to be available well in advance of the agreed time, and that they would wait with the kitchen staff until they were called.

This arrangement turned out to be very beneficial for them, as the head cook had been instructed to serve them with the remains of the game soup from the day before.

'This surely shows that Mistress Mary has kindness of character,' Betty whispered to Molly.

After they had finished, they were called up to be seated just inside the main door. Molly sat with her head half-bowed, as was appropriate, while Betty kept her eyes looking directly in front of her. Then word came that they were to attend Mistress Mary in her bedchamber. They followed the maid up the stairs, and were ushered into a room where the black dresses were laid out on the bed, the patchwork bag beside them. Molly wanted to gaze around to see what kind of room it was, but she knew that she must concentrate only upon the dresses and their owner.

Mistress Mary entered the room, and she appeared much as Molly had imagined her to be. Although a little taller than she and Betty had guessed, she certainly had a slender form, and Molly noted that she moved quite gracefully. She was wearing a simple black dress that surely must have been created specifically to obliterate any signs of her personality.

When Mistress Mary spoke, her voice was clear and gentle, and Molly could see that she had kindness in the expression on her face.

'I trust you ate well,' she began. 'I asked you here because I do not yet go out. I have already examined your work, and I can see the quality of it. My mother was right to use your services, Betty. You must be a good teacher, as your assistant has been able to replicate your skills.'

Betty tried to bob, but the pain in her knees defeated her, and she lowered her head instead.

By quickly turning to the dresses, Mistress Mary contrived not to notice this, an action which Betty greatly valued. Betty and Molly helped her to remove the severe black dress that she was wearing, and as Molly handled it, she was aware of its rough texture, reminiscent of feed sacks. Why had Mistress Mary been forced to wear such a garment, when for someone of her status there was no need? Resolutely, she pushed these thoughts to one side, as the subject was none of her business. Deftly, she aided Betty in the task of helping Mistress Mary into the first of her new dresses. What a transformation! Although also black, even without the addition of the lace the wonderful material seemed to make her body come alive before Molly's very eyes.

Betty drew the attention of Mistress Mary to the long mirror in the corner of the room, bringing it out of the shadows and into full daylight near the window.

When she looked at herself in it, Mistress Mary gasped, and her hand flew to her mouth involuntarily. Then she gathered herself by taking a breath and settling her shoulders, after which she asked Betty to begin making any necessary adjustments.

Betty bustled about, pinching and tacking parts of the bodice. She noted the thinness of Mistress Mary's upper arms, but made no comment, and decided to leave room for some expansion. It was her intuition that the last months in her mother's company had not been conducive to good appetite, and that while staying here, this problem might be rectified. Molly aided Betty attentively, watching her every move, determined to learn everything.

When she had almost completed the work on that dress, Betty said, 'Mistress Mary, I have left plenty of length in the skirts. I trust you will let me know at the next fitting how you want them to lie. An' the lace will be in place by then.'

'Ah, the lace,' said the Mistress. 'You were wise not to have it here today. My brother obtained it from a merchant who recently returned from France. It is very fine. Such lace cannot be got hereabouts.'

Betty nodded in response. Skilfully she directed Molly in how to assist in the removal of the dress, and together they put the other dress on their employer. This fitting did not require the same amount of work, since they had fashioned the two dresses to be well-nigh identical.

Their work complete, they helped Mistress Mary to put on her former attire, and gathered up their things. Thus far, the Mistress had not addressed Molly directly. Molly would have neither expected nor wanted this, but as she retreated to the door of the chamber in advance of Betty's departure, the Mistress said to her, 'Your work as an assistant is excellent.' Then she turned to Betty and said, 'I hope that you will continue to have her in your employ. I shall place another order as soon as this is complete. The servant will deliver the dresses back to you directly. You may leave now.'

Her head bowed, Molly disappeared out of the room, and Betty scuttled backwards to join her. She said nothing until they were well clear of the building.

'Bless you, Molly!' she exclaimed in a low voice, as she hobbled along as fast as she could on her aching knees.

Molly wished that they had brought a stick for Betty, and she tried her best to support her, but Betty shook her hands from her arm impatiently, and struggled on.

In the privacy of the little workroom, she sat down with a grunt, and rubbing her knees, she said, 'Molly, the Mistress was well pleased with our work. She has already promised more, and I can see she has got a liking for you.' Here Betty clutched her hands together and raised her eyes to the ceiling in gratitude. 'We will have a cup of something, and then we will get back to work. Look to see if the servant is coming yet.'

At the door, Molly could indeed see the servant approaching, and she waited, took the bundles from him, and put them safely in the workroom. A shiver of excitement ran through her body as she contemplated the completion of these dresses and the order for other garments, as yet unnamed.

Chapter Eight

As they went about their work, Sam, James and Alec heard many rumours about Mistress Mary. Some thought that she would live at the Master's house forever, whereas others stuck to the original story of her being there only for a few months. Some whispers went about that there were those who sought her hand in marriage, although no one had any idea who might be pursuing her.

At first she was rarely seen outside the house, and she spent much time in her room. However, once her new dresses were finished and had been delivered to her, she was often observed taking walks, either with the Master or closely followed by one of his most trusted male servants.

Betty had received instructions from her that she required several important items of clothing as soon as possible, insisting that Molly was to be fully involved in their creation.

'As if I would keep it all to myself,' Betty grumbled as she and Molly sat mending the farrier's shirts. 'Molly, you an' me have a good way of going about things together, and 'tis to the advantage of us both. Mistress Mary need not worry about who is making her finery.' She lowered her voice. 'An' I have been told not to breathe a word about what we are making. We have to behave as if 'tis more clothes for mourning, when in truth 'tis not.'

Molly was startled. What was this that Betty was telling her? She had imagined that they would be making a black coat next. Maybe instead they were to make a riding skirt?

Betty went on. 'The materials will be delivered here under cover of dark, in a few weeks' time.' She leaned forward in her chair. 'Molly, you must be sure not breathe a word,' she emphasised.

Molly stared at Betty with wide eyes. Betty must indeed be overwhelmed with the responsibility of the Mistress' requests to have said such a thing. Molly was all too aware that she was still quite unable to speak, but even if she could, she would ensure that she guarded the Mistress' secrets well. After all, her future as a seamstress depended on it. She had heard Sam, James and Alec speak of the rumours about possible suitors for the Mistress, and Sam had told her himself in bed at night. But she had discounted them. After all, the Mistress had been devoted to her mother, and her mourning had hardly begun.

The baby that was growing inside Molly had made it necessary for her to make more room in her skirt to accommodate it, and she smiled inwardly, knowing that yet more would be needed. Her child's movements had grown familiar, and she liked to imagine its endeavours, making itself ready for the world outside.

Late one evening some three weeks later, there was a knock at the farrier's door.

'Quick! Snuff the candle,' Betty told her husband.

Knowing what this meant, he followed her instruction, and then made his way to the door in the pitch dark. In the light of the moon outside, the farrier could see that there were two cloaked figures, in charge of three sacks. Nothing was said. The load was passed inside, together with a letter. Then the callers disappeared into the night.

The farrier stacked the sacks in Betty's workroom, and closed the door. He lit the candle again. He knew better than to ask questions. This was the business of women, and he put it out of his mind.

Eager to see Molly again the next day, Betty slept only lightly that night.

Early the following morning, she stationed herself at the front of the house as soon as the farrier left for work. Warmed by the rays of the early sun, she listened to the sounds of bees as they explored the flowers of the honeysuckle that twined on the nearby fence, and tumbled over an old broken cart beyond. Tired, she shut her eyes, and was soon fast asleep.

That was how Molly found her when she arrived. She was seated motionless on a stool, with her back against the wall and her head dropped down. When Molly first saw her, her chest was gripped with fear. When her mother had died, this had been how she had been found, although Molly herself had not been there to see it.

Molly heard a voice cry 'Betty!' in tones that she could not recognise as she ran to the gate and up the path to take Betty in her arms. Sam was only one pace behind her, and he caught Betty's sleeping frame as Molly's grasp disturbed her balance.

Betty woke with a start and began flailing her arms about in alarm.

'Get off!' she screamed.

'It is all right, Betty,' Sam soothed. 'You must have fallen asleep.'

Betty rubbed her eyes, and then peered in turn at Molly and Sam in order to satisfy herself that she was with people she knew.

Tears of relief welled up in Molly's eyes, and she tried to brush them away as they ran down her cheeks. But as fast as she cleared them, more came.

James and Alec stood watching this scene in amazement. They had heard Molly call Betty's name. Molly's voice was a sound that they had not heard in many a long month, and at times had despaired of ever hearing again. To Alec it was like the sound of long-lost music. He turned to James, but his brother seemed to be in a kind of trance.

Sam took Betty's arm and helped her into the house, with Molly following close behind.

This seemed to bring James to his senses, and he turned to Alec and asked, 'Did you hear Molly speak?'

'Aye.'

They said nothing more to one another, but stood quietly at the gate. They did not have long to wait, for Sam appeared after only a few minutes. He touched each of them lightly on the arm, and they carried on along their way to the now partly-built cottages.

'Did she say more?' asked James urgently.

'Nothing more,' Sam replied. 'And I said nothing to her about it.'

'Why not?' asked Alec impatiently.

The way he spoke was out of character, and Sam put his arm across Alec's shoulders as they walked along together. 'Brother,' he said slowly, 'I cannot be certain that she knows she spoke.'

Alec shook Sam's arm away. 'That should make no difference,' he stated emphatically. 'Why did you not just tell her? Then she would have known.' He quickened his pace, and Sam and James let him walk ahead.

That morning, Alec worked in sullen silence, barely stopping to mop his brow as the heat of the day built up. In contrast, Sam was in a jovial mood. His hopes had been raised, and his plans for the future were now coloured with the imagined sound of Molly's happy laughter, something he had missed for far too long. At last they would be able to put behind them the memory of that terrible night last December.

Sam tried his best to jerk Alec out of his silent state, at times using jesting that they had shared as boys. But nothing helped, and he kept his attention focussed on the work and an occasional exchange with James.

James was in a quandary. He was glad to see Sam's happiness, but he was not at all convinced that any permanent change had taken place in Molly. He feared that Alec was more aware of the real situation than was Sam, and he wondered how to help Sam to see this. As he turned the whole problem over in his mind, he decided that it was useless to try to convince Sam of the likely truth, and instead he concentrated his energies on his work.

Noon came, and they sat down to consume the food that had been brought to them.

Sam was restless. He took a bite or two, and then announced, 'I am going to see my Molly.'

But as he stood up, Alec sprang to his feet and said, 'Sam, she will give no other sign.'

Sam glared at him.

Then James spoke. 'I fear Alec is right. Sam, there have been times when I have been convinced I heard Molly speak a word, but it has never led to anything more.'

Sam did not seem to understand. 'But it was real!' he shouted.

James put a finger to his lips. 'Do not let others hear,' he warned.

'It was real,' Sam repeated in a desperate voice. 'I heard her speak.'

James looked at him sadly. 'Yes, you heard her speak. This is the first time for you, and it has raised your hopes.'

Sam glowered at James. 'Why did you not tell me when she spoke before,' he demanded angrily.

'Sam, I wanted to be sure before I spoke to you about it, and I have not yet been certain.'

Sam sat down heavily on a rock, and his body slumped forwards. He put his head in his hands and wailed 'When, oh when will my Molly speak to me again?'

His brothers let him be, as they knew instinctively that he was not yet ready to listen to anything more they had to say.

Sam sat there for a long time. James and Alec finished eating, drank deeply from the water that had been provided, and silently began work once more. It was a while before Sam joined them. When he did, his face was set, and he worked with the strength of more than two men.

Betty felt confused, and lacking in energy. She longed for a cup of her best camomile tea, but did not feel ready to make it. Not only had she slept little that night, but also the excitement of the secret delivery itself had stirred her beyond her normal capacities. She realised that she must have dozed while waiting for Molly's arrival, and when she had come to full consciousness it had been with an unpleasant jolt. She thought that the others could have been concerned by her somnolence. Had they perhaps mistaken it for something sinister? And... she had dreamed that Molly had called her name.

She remained seated in the workroom where Sam had left her, with Molly silently by her side. She did not yet have the strength to speak about the sacks that were piled against the far wall, and Molly made no move to examine them.

At length, Molly touched Betty's arm, and pointed to herself and then to the door.

'Some camomile tea,' Betty requested.

Molly nodded. She left the room, and Betty soon heard her moving things in the kitchen. She heaved a sigh of relief and closed her eyes. A cup of her special tea would surely put her right.

When Molly returned, Betty took the cup and sipped gratefully from its contents. Ah! Molly had brewed it perfectly. Betty savoured every drop of the restoring beverage.

The drink finished, Betty handed the empty cup to Molly to return safely to the kitchen. Betty then took her scissors and worked to open the ties of the uppermost sack.

'Now, you must not breathe a word of what you see,' she instructed briskly. Then she paused, turned to Molly, looked her straight in the eyes, and added slowly and deliberately, '... when you can speak again.'

Molly looked startled, and Betty could see her eyes cloud over in confusion. For a moment she regretted what she had said, but then, believing in the rightness of it, she went on. 'Molly, for all these months you have made but few sounds, but I fancy that this very morning you called my name.'

Molly shook her head vehemently, as if to deny what Betty was saying.

Betty continued unchecked, but her voice was kind and gentle. 'You can speak, but you think you cannot. You called my name today, but you do not remember. The terrible thing that happened to you in December took your voice from you, but you do not have to be like this for the rest of your life.'

Molly clutched at her throat, but Betty took her hands and pulled them to her.

'Do not worry about that for now. What you need to think about is what was stolen from you. Molly, you will need your voice for your child and for your work. You have a good life ahead of you with Sam, James, Alec and the little one.' She waited, and then finished by adding emphatically, 'Think about it, Molly. That is what you have to do next.'

Molly was by now very pale. She swayed on her feet, and Betty feared that she might fall. But then she righted herself, and sat down heavily.

Betty patted her shoulder and said, 'I will get on with opening these sacks.'

Although a little fearful about Molly's state, she turned her back determinedly. Her incisive action was rewarded, as Molly joined her, holding the mouth of the second sack steady. Betty used both hands to loosen its ties, taking great care not to damage the contents.

Then she let Molly look closely inside the two opened sacks. She could see Molly's eyes shining as she tugged at a corner of the material inside the first sack. It was a deep ruby red – a colour rarely seen. Betty watched in delight as the pleasure spread across Molly's face. She laid her cheek against the material, and closed her eyes, savouring its texture. Betty did not hurry her. It was good to see her thus engaged.

When Molly opened her eyes again, she smiled at Betty, and then pointed to the second sack for permission to investigate its contents. Betty nodded, and Molly eagerly engaged with her task, revealing emerald green fabric of a quality she had never before seen, let alone touched. She threw her hands up in delight, and then put a piece against her cheek.

Betty freed the ties on the third sack, and together they discovered white silks and satins and coloured threads inside. By now, Betty was as excited as Molly. They looked at each other, their eyes gleaming.

'An' I have instructions from the Mistress,' Betty told Molly excitedly. She produced the letter from where she had concealed it in the pocket of her apron, and handed it to Molly. 'Read it.'

Molly opened the letter and studied it. She had been lucky to be reared at the doctor's house, as this had meant that she had begun to acquire the skill of reading at an early age. The handwriting was clearly formed, and it was easy to make out what it said. When she had finished it, she handed it back to Betty, well-pleased with what they had been asked to do.

It was only then that Betty realised they had a considerable problem. Her own reading skills were not up to deciphering the letter, their work for Mistress Mary was secret, and Molly could not tell her what they had been asked to do. Betty almost lost patience with Molly, very nearly berating her. With a great effort, she held her tongue, telling herself that the problem was as much due to her own lack of education as to do with Molly's limitation. She would have to be resourceful, and find a way to solve the problem that affected them both. But what could she do?

Then Betty gathered herself and asked, 'Molly, can you make patterns for what Mistress Mary desires?'

Molly was perplexed. Why was Betty asking her to do something that she could well do herself? She could certainly shape something to suit the instructions in the letter, but surely Betty could accomplish the task much better? Betty was very experienced, while Molly knew herself to be a novice, requiring to work under Betty's supervision at all times. How could she possibly take charge of this? It was inconceivable.

Full of uncertainty, she indicated to Betty that she would like to go outside. Although unable to see how this would help them, Betty was willing to do this, and they went together. Betty took up her position sitting against the wall of the house, while Molly searched around at a little distance. When she had found a pointed stick, she began to scratch in the soft earth near Betty's feet.

At first Betty could not make out what Molly was trying to do, but when she saw the shape of a petticoat appear in front of her, she sat bolt upright and exclaimed, 'Bless you, Molly! I cannot read the letter, but you are making it into the kind of writing I can understand.'

Molly nodded. Now sure of what was needed, she went on drawing. At times Betty would stop her and ask questions, and Molly would adapt her illustrations until Betty understood exactly what the letter had said.

Satisfied that she was aware of what Mistress Mary desired, and confident that she and Molly had found a way of communicating about this and any other letter from the Mistress, Betty's mood changed from being near defeat to a kind of triumph.

'Let me think about what you have shown me, and tomorrow we will make a start,' she declared.

By the time they collected Molly from Betty's house, Sam had already accepted that there would be no change in Molly's ability to speak. He kissed her forehead, but then he turned away and walked silently towards the moor. James and Alec took up positions on either side of Molly, and thus escorted her home. She did not appear to perceive Sam's behaviour as being anything out of the ordinary, and seemed happy to have the two brothers as her companions.

That evening, Sam was morose and withdrawn, but Molly's behaviour was unaffected by his mood. Before retiring that night, James tapped Sam on the shoulder and beckoned him outside. At first Sam refused, but when James persisted, he followed him, although with obvious reluctance.

They were barely outside when Sam said irritably, 'What?'

James looked at him quizzically in the half-light and said nothing.

Sam shrugged his shoulders and made as if to go back into the cottage, but James caught his arm. 'Alec and I are of one mind about this,' he began.

Sam made a dismissive gesture, but waited.

'Molly does not know when she has spoken, and until she does, there is no likelihood of her progressing with it,' James stated bluntly.

Sam looked as if his brother had hit him with a heavy object. He became unsteady on his feet, and he reached for the wall of the cottage and collapsed against it.

''Tis too much.'

James reached out and put a warm lingering hand on Sam's shoulder. This gave Sam strength, and he straightened himself. They stood together for a minute or so, and then saying nothing more, they went back into the cottage.

Out of habit, Sam scrutinised Molly's silent frame. Enveloped in her own world, she appeared entirely unaffected by his temporary absence, and was sewing a tiny garment.

That night Sam found himself able to caress her expanding abdomen in a warm embrace as together they drifted off to sleep.

Chapter Nine

Molly rose early the next morning. The air was damp, but mild. She thought it must have rained in the night. She remained very close to the cottage as she waited for the men to wake. She remembered only too well their great distress on the day when she had strayed and they believed that she had been taken from them. Her heart felt light, and the days felt full of promise. It was now clear that Mistress Mary trusted them completely, as if she and Betty were maids who had served her for many years. Although the new work was still a secret, this, and the trust she had placed in them, constituted a great honour.

As she waited, she put both her hands on her growing abdomen. She could feel the changes in its shape when her baby moved. It was already the beginning of September. Her baby had more growing to do, but it would not be many more weeks before she would see her son's face. She was certain that the child would be a boy. Sam needed a son, and he should have one.

Alec was the first to stir, and when he saw her, he joined her. Together they watched the delicate swirls of the rising mist and the swift flight of the pretty birds that swooped to drink where water had collected in depressions formed in the compacted earth that surrounded their cottage.

At the first sign of a cold night, Molly knew that the leaves on the trees would begin to change to their autumn colours. She glanced across to those that clustered round the remains of the old ruin. They had grown much since her childhood. She had first seen them when her mother had been called to attend a pedlar woman who was giving birth in the shelter of one of the walls. She remembered well the filthy stranger who had come to the door, and her mother's unwillingness to go with him. The doctor had been called away early that morning, and would not be back until the next day. Then by chance the old shepherd had hobbled into sight. Her mother had called to him, and was finally persuaded to help the stranger when the shepherd pledged his assistance. The stranger took them all as fast as the shepherd could walk to where the woman lay, and together her mother and the shepherd had relieved the woman of a girl child, born

monster's evil spirit invaded Molly's throat, and stuck there? This was a likely explanation. Why had she not thought of it before? The answer to that was clear – everyone had been filled with gladness about Molly carrying a child, and she had been focussing her energies on teaching Molly to become a seamstress. It was only now that she had time to look into this worrying subject. If she could find a spell to free Molly's voice even a little, then she could teach her how to recognise that she had spoken, and then life itself would heal the rest. The washerwoman's legs had been very weak when she first moved them again, but daily practice had eventually led to them being restored completely.

Betty's mind was made up. A spell it had to be. But she would have to obtain sound advice. Now, whom could she trust? Having got thus far, Betty promised herself that she would give that question due consideration, but that for now, she would concentrate her attention entirely upon the ruby-red dress for the rest of the day.

She turned to Molly. 'I've been thinking those rumours about the Mistress may well have some substance,' she confided. 'There must be someone in pursuit of her hand.'

Molly smiled, and nodded vigorously.

'Well, we're going to make her look even more lovely than in her black attire,' Betty declared confidently. Then a shadow fell across her face as she struggled with the situation. 'If her mother is hardly yet cold in her grave, she cannot in all truth wear anything but black for at least a year, and yet it seems she wants these garments directly.' Here she corrected herself. 'At least, as soon as we can provide them.' She mulled over these conflicting facts for a while. Then she lowered her voice to a near-whisper. 'I can only guess that there is to be a secret assignation, but that the timing of it is dependent upon our output.' Her whisper took on a note of conspiracy. 'Perhaps until then letters are being exchanged.' She coughed, and her voice returned to its usual strength. 'Molly, I very much hope she has given away that gown she wore when she first arrived. A serving maid would be lucky to own such attire, but it is entirely unsuitable for her own use.'

That evening, Betty asked her husband if he would agree to Molly's giving birth under his roof. He made it very clear that he would not fall in with this plan, and although Betty tried hard, he would not be persuaded. It was fine to have Molly working there through the days, but he wanted no disturbance that could stretch into the evening or the night.

Thus Betty's idea was thwarted, but she pledged inwardly not to give up. Next she would speak to her husband's widowed sister, who lived less than a mile away northwards, and her cottage was not much further from the Master's house than was the farrier's. Her sons had left several years ago to seek their fortunes, and she had heard little of them since.

Next she turned her mind to devising a spell. Of course, this would have nothing to do with witchcraft, but to ensure that there was no risk of such a dangerous misapprehension, she decided after all to tell no one of her plan. The spell that she had made for Jane's future had worked very well. Jane was securely settled. Betty smiled as she thought of the peg dolls that she had made. She had dressed them in wedding attire, concealing them under her pillow, and thinking intensely of the kind of suitor she had wanted for Jane. And all the while, whenever she could not be overheard, she had repeated the special words that she had devised. She had been more than pleased to find that her efforts were rewarded within the year.

She would now make two more dolls – one for Molly as she was, and one for Molly as she would be, once her voice was restored. She would conceal them, and every night she would say... What would she say? She must decide upon this quite soon.

Satisfied with her progress, Betty made herself ready for bed.

Chapter Ten

Alec and James took every opportunity to talk to one another about their pact. They wondered if they were ill-advised to do this without consulting Sam, but the more they spoke together, the more they decided against including him. He appeared so much calmer about his situation, and they feared that such discussion would shatter his newly-acquired peace.

The first thing to do was to cast around for information and tales – anything that might contain a fragment of the puzzle. Men from the quarry were the only other contacts that they had, and although they saw some of them each day, neither James nor Alec had close contact with them. But they agreed that since these men were a potential source, they would now devise a way of spending more time in their proximity.

On the pretext of placing closer supervision on the workings of the quarry, James arranged to spend some mornings there over the following week. After that, he exchanged places temporarily with a young man known by the name of Thomas, who was keen to acquire building skills. Alec and Sam found Thomas to be an able and energetic apprentice.

By the end of the second week, James' scheme had yielded well. He had introduced new ways of handling the stone, and he planned to ask the Master if they could keep Thomas on as an apprentice builder, and find a replacement for him at the quarry. As well as all of this, he had overheard something that he wanted to discuss with Alec urgently.

On the way home that evening, James contrived to let Molly and Sam go ahead, and since this was not unusual, it did not cause comment.

As soon as he was sure that they were out of earshot, he turned to Alec and said, 'At the quarry today I overheard two of the men whispering to each other about a curse.'

'A curse?' Alec was alarmed. In his life, he had heard several stories of curses, all of which had involved the kind of consequences he would not want to endure.

'Aye, a curse.'

Alec's instinct warned him that he did not want to hear anything about this curse. His experience thus far had been that knowledge of curses should be avoided. Yet his intuition battled with this belief, and he urged James to tell him what he had learned.

'I heard them speak of a man who had been struck down with an illness that robbed him of his speech. All he could do was mumble.'

Alec's anxiety led him to interrupt. 'Our Molly does not mumble.'

'Be patient, Alec. There is more to this tale,' said James quietly.

Alec fell silent, and James continued. 'It had been a good while before he could make much sound.'

Alec interrupted again. 'When was this?'

'I could not determine exactly. I thought it important not to show my interest. But I think it was many years ago.'

Alec felt less agitated, and fell silent once more.

'I stayed close to the one who told this tale, listening as hard as I could. There were many questions I wanted to ask, but I had to rely only upon what his friend asked.'

'Go on, James. Go on,' Alec urged.

'I think I heard a mention of huge hands.'

Alec stopped dead in his tracks. 'Huge hands!' He swivelled round and grabbed James by the front of his shirt. 'Tell me everything!' he shouted.

James made no move to resist his brother's grasp. He knew only too well how he must be feeling at this moment. His own impulses had directed him to grab the bearer of the story, and drag him to see Alec and Sam, but his heart had told him that this was likely only to result in disorder. Such disturbance might have cost him his job, and in addition yield less of the information he so sorely desired to obtain, so he had stayed his hand.

Alec's arms dropped to his sides, and he bowed his head. 'I did not mean...' His voice trailed off, and James put a hand on his shoulder before they resumed their journey.

'The only other thing I heard was of the curse, but I cannot be certain of the facts.'

Alec walked on with his brother, giving him time to find the words.

'The curse is in the stone.'

Alec wanted to scream. He had to know the answers to the

questions that flooded his mind. What stone? What were the words of the curse? Who had spoken it? How had it impregnated the stone? Where had the stone come from? Where had it travelled? Where was the stone now?

James' voice was tight as he recounted his experience. He spoke through clenched teeth. 'I wanted to grab the man who was speaking and pin him with his back against the rock face. I wanted to keep him there until I knew everything, but I knew that I must not.'

'You were right, James,' Alec reassured him quietly. His heart and mind seethed, yet reason kept hold of them. 'Is there anything else you can tell me?'

'The man's friend asked him for the words of the curse.'

Alec leaned towards James in anticipation.

'But the man refused, saying that the danger was too great. He said that it was believed that the words had such power as to have killed any man who tried to pass them on.'

Alec moaned. 'If our dear Molly is in the grip of the effects of this, we are even more lucky that she lives than we first thought.'

James nodded. 'That came to my mind too.'

'James, you did well. I had wished I was there with you, but I would not have behaved in a right way.'

'Another thing happened. I thought that the man who wanted to know the curse was not just asking from curiosity. The words he spoke were innocent enough, but the tone of his voice and the slyness of the near-concealed expression on his face alerted me. This helped me not to interfere. If that man wanted the curse for evil intent...'

Here Alec could not but interrupt. 'Brother, you could have done no better. Above all you must keep yourself safe. Life without you cannot be imagined, let alone borne.' He thought for a while, and then his voice took on a new strength. 'Together we will find the means to discover more.'

'I think I should work at the quarry a little longer.'

'Aye, your time there might bring more fruit. We are making good progress at the cottages despite your absences and Thomas' lack of experience. The Master will not complain if you are at the quarry for another few mornings.'

James savoured these thoughts, and then said, 'The men have grown accustomed to my presence. At first they were wary, but now they barely give me a glance unless I approach them directly. Now is the time to work more closely alongside them.'

Chapter Eleven

By the end of September, Betty had secured an agreement with her sister-in-law that Molly could give birth at her cottage. The next thing would be to speak to the cook to see if she were willing to assist, and once that was accomplished, Betty would have to find a way to ask the Master if he might release cook for such a duty. Putting this request in front of him was no easy matter for someone of her station. A direct approach from her would not be acceptable. Betty searched her mind for a way, but could think of nothing.

Secretly she had completed the two peg dolls, and had concealed them under her horsehair pillow. There was no risk that her husband would find them, as she alone was responsible for the care of the bed.

Betty had put much thought into the wording of the spell, and had eventually fixed upon a system that satisfied her. She repeated it silently every night before she fell asleep. *Wickedness be gone. Let Molly's voice be mended.*

James' presence had become so familiar at the quarry that the men's tongues loosened about all kinds of things. They knew that he would cause them no harm for the simple act of passing a story or a jest between them. In fact, James had noticed that such behaviour generally resulted in greater output, and so although he did not encourage the men into it, he certainly did not deter them. Most of their chatter was of no concern to him, but he listened out at all times.

At the end of one morning, when he was about to pack up and return to join Sam, Alec and Thomas, he heard something that instantly alerted him. He turned his head a little, and spied the man who had had a sly look on his face when asking about the curse. He was talking to a young man who had recently come into the Master's employ.

'Aye, my grandfather told me something of the same,' he heard the young man say.

The sly man said, 'I once knew that curse.'

James could tell that the sly one was lying.

'I never asked what it was,' said the young man.

The sly man was cunning. 'Ah,' he said, 'it irks me that I cannot pull it back up into my mind.'

James could see that the young man was eager to impress the sly one, who was some years older than he.

'I could ask my grandfather,' the young man offered. 'He will be at the church on Sunday.'

'I might have remembered by then, but if not, I'd be pleased if you would,' the sly man replied.

James noted the apparently casual way in which he said these words, but he knew for certain that this was a subterfuge. He tied up his belongings in a sack, threw it over his shoulder and strode off, whistling cheerfully to conceal his conflict. He wanted mischief to befall the sly man before he had chance to learn the secret, and he wanted to protect the young man and his grandfather, while learning anything that could be of help to Molly.

When he neared the cottages, he saw that Alec and Sam were working closely together, with Thomas at a distance. He wished passionately that he could replace Alec with Thomas, so that he could give him the news straight away, but he would have to wait at least until they crossed the moor, and possibly even later.

It was late in the evening before James had his chance. Sam and Molly were having a conversation – Molly again using the ashes as her voice. He touched Alec's arm, and they stepped outside together.

James breathed deeply from the balmy air. The moon shone brightly, and the evening temperature was barely beginning to fall. Thus far, this month had been exceptionally mild, and the trees still carried many of their now multicoloured leaves. He beckoned to Alec to join him at a distance from the door.

'You have news?' asked Alec in a low voice.

James told him what he had witnessed, and Alec drew a quick breath to stifle his gasp.

'This day is Friday,' said James. 'I will return to the quarry tomorrow and I will speak to the young man, but first I must devise a plan of ridding us of the sly one.'

'You cannot kill him,' stated Alec forthrightly.

'I can, but I must not,' James corrected him. 'I should send him on an errand... from which he cannot return.'

'What can that be?'

James' thoughts flowed swiftly. 'He must be offered a lure. He must be plied with drink. There is no doubt he will fall for that. Then

I will send him on an errand to the Master's house, where he will make a fool of himself and be sent packing.'

'But we have no such drink,' said Alec.

'There is a little at the cave,' James informed him.

Alec was astonished. 'I have not seen it. Where did you conceal it?'

Amusement spread across James' face. 'It is hidden well, in a cavity at the back, with a stone to hide it. I will go by way of the cave in the morning, and then travel quickly to intercept my prey before he reaches the quarry.' He spat in his hand and held it out to his brother. Alec did the same, and they joined hands, thus reaffirming their pact.

ignorance, and begged his forgiveness. He told me to keep well clear of that man. I have been saved from him by his absence.'

'He will not be back.'

James had spoken with such certainty that the young man did not question him. Instead he said, 'My grandfather told me that since the curse was placed in the stone, it has moved with the stone, and each time the stone has been moved, another has fallen prey to the curse.'

'Does he know the words of the curse?'

The young man nodded. 'He says they will never be spoken again, and that they will die with him.'

'So that will prevent the curse from being spread about,' James acknowledged. 'But how can its power in the stone be halted? And if it is this that has affected our dear Molly, how are we to reverse that damage?' James had to struggle to ensure that his voice did not rise to a wail.

The young man put a hand lightly on his arm before jumping to his feet. 'I will speak to you again,' he said. Then he bounded back to the rock face, and resumed his work.

'Well, Molly,' Betty began. 'There is a puzzle here.'

Molly tipped her head to one side to indicate a question in her mind.

'How are we going to let the Mistress know that her dress is ready?'

Molly had not thought of this before, and she could tell that neither had Betty. They had both been so excited by the project that they had concentrated only upon its completion, and not upon the consequence of that.

'I could hobble up to the house, but everyone would know that something was afoot. I could ask my husband to fetch a servant, but it would have to be the right one, and I know not whom to ask for. I cannot write, so 'tis not possible to send a letter.' Then a thought occurred to her. 'We could send a scrap of the material to her. Surely she would know what that meant. That's it! I shall send a scrap with my husband. He can give it to the cook. She will know how to ensure that it finds its way safely to the Mistress.'

James was subdued when he spoke to Alec in a quiet moment late that afternoon. When James recounted the events of the morning to him, Alec felt very nervous, and more than once looked behind him as

James was speaking.

Molly was in good spirits when the three brothers collected her from Betty's that afternoon. Despite her bulk, she danced a few steps playfully from time to time, and teased each of them by tweaking the hair in their beards, always catching them by surprise.

Chapter Thirteen

In the event, Betty did not have to put her plan into action, as the Mistress herself called on her the next day. Betty was startled when she heard the knocking.

'Mercy me!' she exclaimed. 'Whoever can that be?' She stood up stiffly, and made her way slowly to the door. When she saw the Mistress standing there, she could not speak.

'Good morning, Betty,' said Mistress Mary. 'I have heard that you make an excellent cup of camomile tea. I should like to sample it while I rest on this stool at your door.'

Betty attempted to bob, and nearly fell. She clutched at the doorframe and steadied herself, and then managed to say, 'I will bring you a cup directly.'

Betty returned as quickly as she could, shuffling along the passageway, lest she stumble and spill the tea. She handed the cup to Mistress Mary, who held her nose close to it and breathed in deeply.

'Ah, 'tis surely of excellent quality,' she pronounced. 'Come, sit with me while I drink.'

Betty settled herself on the edge of the other stool, which stood a few feet away, and she could see a servant waiting at a distance. She presumed that he was attending the Mistress, as she should not be walking alone.

Mistress Mary took a small sip, and held it in her mouth to savour it before swallowing.

'There must be magic in this,' she decided. 'Camomile alone cannot taste so heavenly.'

Betty hastened to assure her that the drink contained only her best camomile, gathered and dried by her own hands.

The Mistress uttered a burst of melodic laughter. 'In that case,' she declared, 'the secret lies in you.'

This was a delight to Betty's ears, and she relaxed and smiled contentedly.

'Come closer,' the Mistress invited.

Thus instructed, Betty lifted her stool, and placed it at the other side of the doorway, only inches away from the Mistress.

'That is much better,' the Mistress approved. Then her voice dropped. 'How is the progress of the red gown?'

''Tis almost complete. At this very moment, Molly is putting the last stitches in it. I had planned to send a scrap of the material for cook to pass to your servant to alert you.'

The Mistress raised her voice. 'That will not be necessary of course.' Then quietly she added, 'I will send someone this very night. Please work on the undergarments next.' Raising her voice again, she announced, 'I am much restored. Do you have more camomile?'

'Aye, that I do. I have enough to last the winter, and more.'

'Well, then, I will call again quite soon. My health will be much the better for it.'

At that, Mistress Mary stood up, beckoned to the servant, and left by the gate.

Betty waited for a respectful time, before hurrying as fast as she could to see Molly.

Her head close to Molly's ear, she whispered, 'Did you hear what she said?'

Molly nodded excitedly, and a smile lit her face. For a moment Betty stopped and considered how throughout her confinement, Molly had seemed to gain in strength and beauty.

Then she enquired briskly, 'It is complete?'

Molly showed her the final neat stitches.

'Then we must pack it directly. After that we will begin to fashion the undergarments.'

Sam noted an air of suppressed excitement in Molly when he collected her at Betty's gate. He could only assume that it was her reaction to the forthcoming birth of their child. She looked lovely. Since her sickness in the early weeks, he had noticed her vitality increasing. The only thing that was missing was her voice. Every day, he longed to talk with her about their baby. She conversed well through signs, symbols and drawings, but his heart ached for the sound of her voice. He had never forgotten that sound. Whenever he had had chance to see her throughout her childhood years, he had drunk in the sound of it, and when her voice had matured, he had stored the precise inflections of it in his mind, from where he could call them up at will. Throughout the long months of her silence, it was upon this that he relied.

As they all crossed the moor together, he realised that there was something different about James and Alec also. He could not quite put his finger on it. He was not sure when it had begun, but there was a definite change. To the eye, they looked the same as always, but to his inner sensings there was definitely something. He could identify no thread of change upon which to remark. He could think of nothing that could be challenged. And yet there was something... If he were to be honest with himself, he supposed that they too might detect a change in him. Although every day he inwardly reaffirmed his vow to destroy the entity that had attacked his Molly, outwardly he took every care to appear as if he were content, and it was this apparent state that he sought to impress upon them. Every day he acknowledged the black hatred in his heart against whatever evil force had damaged her, and yet he showed only warmth in all his dealings with others. As if it were only yesterday, he remembered the pact that he had made with James and Alec, but he never made any mention of it.

Then something came to him with a jolt. If he had become so adept at dissembling about what lay deep in his heart, then his brothers also must have that ability. Aye, this could well account for the inexplicable feelings that he had about them. Molly herself was living two lives – the one that was full of joy, meaning and purpose, and the other that was full of the horror that had robbed her of speech. Sam realised that the consequence of her inability to see this had meant that in his own way he had come to mirror her condition. It would therefore not be surprising if it had affected James and Alec similarly.

Although shaken by this new awareness, in some strange way Sam was also strengthened by it. When he questioned the reason for this latter feeling, he knew that it was because he was facing more of the truth.

In the darkness of that night, there was a sound at the farrier's door. Having been forewarned by his wife, the farrier had stationed himself in the passageway without a light, ready for this visitor. He quickly opened the door, and passed the dress out, cunningly disguised as a sack of meal, to the cloaked figure that waited there. Both men entered into the play by handling the sack as if it weighed more than it truly did, lest some prowler spied them.

The farrier closed the door firmly, and went to his bedchamber. Without pausing to change into his nightgown, he grabbed at Betty and drew her close. Betty, who had been lying wide awake, had suspected that this would be a result of the night's work. Despite her ageing frame, she engaged with him as willingly as she was able. She was glad to serve him thus. After all, she would have to rely on him for clandestine tasks many times in the months to come. He was her sure defence against the eyes of prying neighbours, and the Mistress would be likely to reward them well.

Chapter Fourteen

Thomas had quickly proved to be as willing an apprentice to Sam, James and Alec as Molly was to Betty. The Master had been uncertain about engaging a replacement in his place at the quarry, but as the weeks passed, he made it known that he would do so by Easter the following year.

So used were the brothers to Molly's silence that they barely noticed Thomas' lack of conversation. It was enough for them that he could speak when required. Indeed, Sam knew that he would have found it irksome had Thomas spoken often. He guessed that James and Alec felt the same, but he did not ask them. It was part of the unspoken life that they shared.

James continued his regular visits to the quarry, although they were less frequent, being every second or third morning. When time and strength allowed, the men there continued their banter. It was around that time that James became aware of Thomas' silence. He supposed that he found this welcome, as there was less contrast between Thomas' state and Molly's. James had begun to note that there was a curious similarity between Thomas and the young man at the quarry. Their age, height, and strong, light build were well-nigh the same, although their colouring differed. The young man at the quarry had piercing blue eyes, and fair hair that had bleached in the sun, whereas Thomas had a greenish tinge to his eyes, and his brown hair was unaffected, being always hidden under a knitted cap. James had deliberately not asked the young man his name, as he did not want to treat him differently from the other men. Every day he had longed to speak with him again, but the young man had shown no sign of this being necessary or right. Trusting his integrity, James waited for a signal.

Mistress Mary's second visit to Betty's house came only a week after the first. Every day, Betty had listened out for the slightest sound of her coming, taking Molly into her confidence about this.

For late September, the sun at noon was still warm, and again Mistress Mary took tea on a stool at the door, with Betty seated beside her.

After some pleasantries, the Mistress again lowered her voice, and Betty sensed that deeper confidences were about to be imparted. She looked towards the servant, making as if no conversation were taking place, and listened intently to what the Mistress had to say.

'The dress is perfect. How goes the stitching of the undergarments?'

'The work progresses well,' Betty reported with an air of confidence.

'I have a suitor!' These words were whispered so quietly as if they had not been spoken, but Betty did not doubt what her acute hearing had witnessed. So, she had guessed correctly!

The Mistress continued. Betty glanced across at her, and noted that her lips hardly moved as she spoke. 'I have put complete trust in you. If anyone learns of my situation, I will be denied my status for the rest of my life. Betty, my suitor requires an instant assurance that I am to be his, and yet if I give it, I am lost.'

'Does he know this?' Betty murmured.

The Mistress took a slow, deliberate sip from the cup, and gazed around as if enjoying the scenery. 'Yes, he does. He sent word that if he could see me just once in a dress for which he has provided, he will consider me his, and he will not let it be known that I have broken my mourning. He will wait for me, and will propose to me the day after the anniversary of my mother's death.'

'Your secret has safe haven in this house,' Betty assured her.

'Thank you, Betty,' replied the Mistress in audible tones. 'I will return in one week. This treatment is greatly beneficial to my health.'

She made as if to stand, but on impulse Betty put out a hand to discourage her. But then she flushed, anxious about the possible outcome of her action.

'What is it, Betty?' asked the Mistress kindly.

'I have a worry on behalf of Molly.'

'Then you must tell me what it is.'

'I have the agreement of my sister-in-law to offer her a place there when she is to be delivered, but I need a pair of experienced hands. Would the Master spare the cook on that day?' Betty bowed her head and waited silently. She had stepped into an arena that was quite beyond her station, and the result could be disastrous.

Her fears dispersed when Mistress Mary said, 'I should have thought of that myself. I will speak to my brother this very day.'

Betty looked at her gratefully. The Mistress rose to her feet, and moved gracefully towards the gate.

It was one day in early October when James' patience was finally rewarded. The young man beckoned him to a cart that was standing at a good enough distance from the quarry, and made a play of drawing his attention to something in the wheel assembly.

While they were thus engaged, he whispered, 'My grandfather asks if you took stone from the ruin to build your cottage.'

James replied that they had, and the young man continued.

'He thought that was the case, but asked me to make certain before I passed his message to you.'

James found it hard to contain himself. He could not bear to wait even a second, so great was his longing to procure any information that might result in the healing of Molly's condition. He wanted to grab his informant and force the message out of him instantly. With all his strength he held his arms rigidly by his sides and waited.

The young man's gaze pierced his eyes.

'He told me that you should search the walls of your cottage. You will find a stone that has to be returned to the ruin. This must be done before the birth.'

'But how will I know it?' asked James desperately.

'Fear not. It will come to you.'

At that, the young man went back to his work, leaving James feeling troubled. He left the quarry straight away. He wanted to find Alec and tell him what had taken place. He hurried as fast as he could, and despite the cold October breeze, arrived sweating.

Alec was on the partly-covered roof, but when he saw James coming, he detected that there was something afoot, so he swiftly descended the steps of the wooden ladder and went to meet him.

When James told him what he had learned, Alec wanted to go back to their cottage without delay, to begin the search. Although every part of James' body wanted the same, he persuaded Alec that they should wait. They must not allow anyone to know, and to ensure this they must not change their habits in any way. The afternoons were beginning to draw in, so it would not be long before they could leave with Sam to collect Molly.

On their way home that day, James and Alec could not agree as to whether or not they should take Sam into their confidence.

'He should know,' said Alec determinedly.

'But it would disturb him,' James argued.

Alec persisted. ''Tis his right to know.'

'But Alec, when he hears he is likely to tear the cottage apart.'

Alec considered this deeply before responding. 'You are right. As soon as you told me, that is what I wanted to do. Sam would be the same.'

'And he might not be able to prevent himself from doing so,' James added starkly. 'Molly should have no such disturbance around her.'

'And yet, the message was clear. The stone had to be shifted before she gives birth.'

Alec fell silent for a while, and James let him be, as his own mind was busy with the dilemma.

Presently, Alec spoke again. 'Do we know anything of the likely consequence if we do not find the stone before then?'

'Nothing.'

'Then you must ask the young man at the quarry.'

James agreed to this. 'I shall find the soonest opportunity. Meanwhile we must not tell Sam anything of this.'

'Until we have further word, I'm with you in this, but there will come a time when he must know. Even if we find the stone quite soon, he must be told.'

James sighed. 'I wish not. I fear what it will do to him.'

''Tis his right to know,' Alec reminded him quietly. 'We will have to deal with the consequences.'

Here James acceded. 'For some while we have kept him from his part in the pact. That has been for good reason. I wish with all my heart that we could protect him from this new knowledge, but I know that so doing will cause more damage than it will avoid.'

Alec nodded, and said nothing further about it.

James began to speak of how to go about searching their dwelling. 'It must not be apparent,' he muttered, almost to himself. Then he turned to his brother. 'Alec, I will rise early and search outside.'

'You must fetch me the moment something draws you.'

'That I will,' James promised.

Alec continued. 'For my part, I will begin making such an examination of the inside as can be conducted by candlelight. I can start this very evening.'

'How will you conceal your purpose?'

'Fear not. I have a plan.'

'What is it?'

'Molly's child is soon to be born. What better a project could I embark upon than cleaning the stonework inside our cottage?'

James slapped Alec across the back. 'I will help the others to admire your work.'

'There is but one more thing. We have not set foot in Sam and Molly's room since we finished building it. I cannot see how we can now change that. If we do not find the stone in our other searches, we will have to enter that room.'

'If it becomes necessary, we will find a way,' James replied. His face was set.

Alec was satisfied with this, and said no more.

Their plan devised, the brothers finished their journey in silence.

Alec began his search as soon as he entered their dwelling. Using his knife in one hand and a candle in the other, he started high up in one corner.

'What is this?' asked Sam curiously.

'I have a plan to make ready for the coming of the child,' Alec explained.

'Do you want a hand?' James enquired with a perfectly-contrived air of innocence. 'What is your intention?'

'There are loose fragments on these walls, and I want to clear them away,' Alec told him seriously. 'My knife guides me as to their whereabouts.'

Sam was impressed by Alec's thoughtfulness and his attention to detail, and he offered to work alongside his brothers. But they declined, saying that this was their contribution to the preparations.

After Molly and Sam had gone to their room, Alec and James continued with their scraping, but stood at the opposite end of the cottage. This location, together with the sounds that they made, meant that they could converse quietly without being overheard.

'I have not yet seen anything of note,' Alec reported.

'My own knife has revealed nothing.'

'We have nearly completed a search of half of these inner walls.'

'Tomorrow night will easily finish it, and by then I will have scrutinised much of the outer walls.'

'I must rise with you tomorrow. Daybreak is coming later, and we will have little time before we cross the moor.'

'Alec, if we find something when the others are awake, we must not show any sign.'

'I have been thinking that.'

Just then, something caught Alec's attention. He dug deeply between two stones with his knife.

'What is it?' James questioned eagerly.

'I cannot yet tell. Here, hold the light for me.' Alec passed his candle to James, who held it close to the place. Then Alec used both hands to manoeuvre his blade. After a while, he shook his head. 'Nay, 'tis but a piece of loose stone that is trapped. I fancied it had a different feel to it.'

Tired but not despondent, the brothers snuffed out their candles, and lay down for the night.

Alec woke first. He thought that he could hear alarm amongst the chickens in the enclosure. Maybe a fox had passed by. He saw no reason to hurry out, as the chickens were well-protected by a thick layer of thorny branches that they had woven along and above the fence that contained them. He moved quietly to the door, and as he stood outside he could see faint light creeping into the sky.

Woken by the air that flowed in through the opened doorway, James stretched, rubbed his eyes, and got to his feet. He could see the shape of his brother outside, and he went to join him. Together they watched the sun rise until there was enough light. Then they began to examine the stones. This time they dared not use their knives, as there was no plausible explanation that they could give to Sam and Molly for such action. They worked at opposite ends of the cottage to limit any interest Sam might show if he discovered their activities.

It was Molly who first emerged from the cottage, and she soon saw Alec. Immediately he stopped, and called to her.

'Is Sam ready? Then we must leave.'

James heard him, and came to the door without being observed.

Within minutes, the four were traversing the moor. Molly was in a cheerful mood, and from time to time skipped a step or two. This lifted Sam's spirits, and Alec and James dropped behind the others for a few minutes to communicate that each had found nothing. They planned to continue searching as soon as they returned.

As always, Molly hurried happily through Betty's gate, and disappeared into the house. The atmosphere in the cosy workroom was one of excited conspiracy, and this kept them busily stitching at a good pace.

The others continued on to where Thomas was already up a ladder, making part of the roof fast. This must be completed before there was any danger of high winds or snow. Since the work had advanced, Thomas had taken to sleeping in the shell of one of the row of dwellings. Thus far, October had been almost as mild as September, but it was not wise to expect that this would continue. At this time of year, the weather could change rapidly and unexpectedly for the worse.

Still in high spirits, Sam called to him. Thomas turned and raised a hand, saying nothing before continuing his task. James thought again how alike this was to Molly's behaviour. This, and the similarity in his physical features to the young man at the quarry, made James wonder if there was more to his presence here than merely the excellent work he produced.

That afternoon, James and Alec insisted that they should collect Molly a little earlier. Sam had protested, seeing no reason for hurry, but James and Alec had argued that Thomas was content to carry on alone, and he agreed, albeit reluctantly.

Once back, James and Alec continued the search within their home.

Sam was puzzled. 'There is no need to hurry. Molly's baby will not come yet.'

Alec was ready for this. 'We hope not, but we have heard of births that happened earlier that expected.'

To this Sam acceded, and he said no more.

At the end of that evening, the walls had revealed nothing unusual.

On their mattresses that night, James and Alec whispered to one another.

'The work on the Master's cottages is nearly done,' said James. ''Tis our dwelling that needs our attention.'

'We must find a way of being here in daylight hours,' Alec replied.

'I ache with longing to stay here tomorrow. I am sorely tempted to feign a sickness,' James admitted.

Alec was surprised at his brother's suggestion, but after a moment's thought said deliberately, 'It could be arranged. When you wake in the morning, make no move. I will do the rest.'

The brothers spat into their left hands, and silently joined them in the darkness.

When Sam rose the next morning, he found Alec applying a cloth soaked in cold water to James' forehead.

'He was fevered in the night,' he explained. He hated this subterfuge, and did not look into Sam's eyes. He went on. 'He is past it now, but we should let him rest.'

Sam agreed.

'He will be fine when we return,' Alec added confidently.

As they set off to cross the moor, Alec engaged Sam in conversation about their previous hopes for a bulling heifer. They had learned that the Master had no stock to spare this year, but they were more than happy with the promised grain to see them through the winter. The provision of the chickens had been an unforeseen bonus, and they had laid well. Maybe they would earn a calf in the spring once they had started work on the next row of cottages.

Minutes after the three had left, James sprang to his feet, and immediately continued his search of the outside of their home. By noon he had completed this, finding nothing. All that was left now was the inside of Sam and Molly's room. Without hesitating, he strode into it, and concentrated upon his quest. But again there was nothing.

James struggled with his feelings. Finding nothing was a great relief, but also a great worry. Had he missed something? Or was it that after all none of these stones was affected?

He went outside and sat at the door with his head in his hands. What could he do now? The whole afternoon was ahead of him, and he must make best use of it. This might be the only time that he had to search freely.

It was then that he thought to check the walls of the enclosure. Although not strictly part of their cottage, it was certainly attached to it. If he found nothing, he would walk across to the ruin, and while there he could contemplate what he might do next.

Careful examination of the enclosure led to nothing, and James made his way to the ruin. In recent times nothing further had come to light about its history, and they knew no more about the origin of the stone, or the purpose of the building. Turning these thoughts over in his mind, he found himself mechanically examining every remaining stone that he could find. Some were concealed under dying bracken, whereas others were clearly visible on grassy patches. Something prompted him to make as thorough an examination of these stones as he had of those that they had used for their dwelling. It was because of this impulse that he found something that riveted his attention. On the flat side of half a stone, he could see the impression of what appeared to be a tiny creature. He searched around to find the other half stone, but could not find it anywhere. As if guided, he picked up the half stone, and carried it back to the cottage, where he put it near the fireplace. Then he sat and waited for the others to come home.

He had only an hour to wait before he heard them, and he went outside. Molly was well ahead of the others. She ran to him, and examined his face carefully. Having reassured herself that he was well again, she took his hand and led him inside, making him sit near her while she laid the fire ready to light. It was then that she caught sight of the half stone with its small indent, and as she did, a cry of delight jumped from her throat.

James did not hesitate. He picked up the stone and put it in her hand, and then put her other hand to her throat.

'Molly,' he told her, 'you made a sound. Can you make it again?'

Surprised, Molly tried, but nothing came.

'Try again,' James instructed quietly.

Molly put great effort into this, but there was no sound. She looked upset.

'Never mind,' he comforted her. 'You made a lovely sound.' He looked into her eyes with a serious expression, saying slowly and emphatically, 'You must remember that.'

It was then that Sam and Alec appeared.

'Molly has made a sound,' James told them calmly.

Sam took her in his arms and held her. He knew not to ask anything or press her to repeat the sound.

'We will all remember that this day Molly has made a sound,' said Alec.

Molly stayed close to Sam for a little while. She looked relaxed and pleased, and she kept touching her throat as if in a sense of wonder.

It was only later that she went to her box of carvings, and selected something that she then handed to James. He took it from her and began to study it. Straight away he knew that it would fit exactly into the indent in the half stone in the hearth. For a moment he felt paralysed. What should he do?

Then as if again guided, he turned to Alec and said casually, 'I felt restored this afternoon, and I walked across to the ruin. I picked up this half stone.' He handed it to Alec, pointing to the indent on its face.

'Let me see,' said Sam.

Silently Alec passed it to him.

'A curious indentation,' Sam remarked.

James handed to him the object that Molly had given to him, and Sam fitted it into the face of the rock.

Alec felt that he could not breathe. He wanted to grab that rock and its appendage, and hurl them both as far away from their cottage as he possibly could. James felt a great sickness in the pit of his stomach, and he shut his eyes for a moment in an attempt to still his raging thoughts.

Sam placed the rock and Molly's small piece carefully at the side of the hearth. Separately James and Alec wished fervently that they had told him before of what they knew. What were they to do now?

It was James who seemed to recover first. He addressed Molly.

'I think that I must return my stone to the ruin before we set off across the moor tomorrow. Will you come with me? Perhaps we could leave your piece with it.'

To his great relief, Molly fell in with this suggestion without any hesitation.

James made no attempt to explain anything to Sam, and he was glad to discover that Sam asked for none.

The placing of the stone at the ruin was a simple act that took little time. Molly indicated that she wanted to choose a place to lodge it, and James fell in with this silent request. Turning her back on James, Molly carefully placed it where she had last seen the pedlar woman all those many years ago, and hid the small piece underneath it. After that, they all made their way to Betty's house, where that morning, Mistress Mary had sent a messenger to give Betty the news that the cook's services for Molly's labour had been secured. Betty proudly told Molly straight away. Now everything was in place – a secure house, with enough people in attendance, including a safe pair of hands to deliver the baby. Her only disappointment was that the Mistress herself had not visited them again. Betty longed to learn more of the mysterious suitor, and the only way she could find out was from the Mistress herself. She would have to bide her time, and hope for another visit before the month was out.

Betty stitched at a fine petticoat, her mind full of secret assignations between Mistress Mary and the mysterious suitor, while Molly decorated an underbodice. And true to her promise to herself, every night Betty repeated the words of her spell over the peg dolls that lay under her pillow.

While Molly designed a pleasing decoration on the underbodice, she thought of Mistress Mary's suitor. As she stitched, she hoped that if he saw this decoration it would increase his ardour and commitment to the Mistress. She thought of the sound she knew that she had made last evening, and from time to time, she reached up and touched her throat. And she thought of the poor pedlar woman and her dead child. Then her thoughts turned to all the tiny clothes that she and Betty had made for her baby. Betty had been explicit about her plans for who was to attend the birth and where it should take place, but Molly still knew in her heart that it could only take place in her own home. And yet she accepted that when the time came, fate would decide.

Chapter Fifteen

November had come, with its damp dark days. The Master's row of cottages was complete. The quarry was silent. Mistress Mary's undergarments were finished, and had been taken by night from Betty's house. The Mistress had sent word that she was well pleased with them. Sam, James, Alec and Molly no longer crossed the moor each morning. Betty would begin work on the green dress directly. She would stitch alone until early March, when Molly would come again, bringing her baby with her, an arrangement to which Betty's husband had agreed.

The brothers spent all the daylight hours storing up more fuel for the darkest months. They guarded Molly carefully, and watched her for any small sign that the baby was about to come, as they had the task of taking her safely to Betty's sister-in-law in good time.

Then the dampness turned to a vicious coldness, and the kind autumn turned to harsh winter almost overnight. The cruel wind bent the trees to breaking point. It found the smallest gaps in walls and poured icy air through them. Molly took to stuffing scraps of hide and sacking into the places most affected, in order to prevent the worst of the invasion. Her belly was now so distended that she frequently collided with things when she least expected it, and she often moved with her hand on it to shield it.

Next the snow began. It did not sprinkle the landscape with a pretty sparkling covering. Instead it poured down ceaselessly, forming a thick blanket, silencing everything. At first, opening the door was hazardous, as the merciless gale would force a section of the piled snow right into their living space. Molly and the brothers could not remember a November like this. As more and more snow collected, the cottage was engulfed, and the brothers had to tunnel their way to the outside. At that stage it became very obvious to them all that unless the weather changed back to a milder state very soon, Molly's baby would be born here.

The days passed slowly. They whiled away the hours with their games and stories, and Molly took up her carving once more.

Then one day in the last week of the month, Molly saw a piece of blood-streaked mucus appear on her leg. She showed it to Sam, who immediately understood its significance, and spoke to James and Alec.

It was not until the next day that Molly began to feel something strange and unfamiliar. At first it felt as if some part of her belly was drawing itself in, without her applying any conscious effort. She placed a hand where she had felt it most, and when that squeezing feeling came again, she could detect the change with her touch. This repeated from time to time until she became used to it, and she found herself anticipating the next one with a breath of excitement. As she grew more familiar with her state, she took Sam's hand so that he could feel that squeezing too. She watched his face as he discovered this new magic, and then saw it soften during the hours that followed, while he waited for signs of further change. As he became sufficiently accustomed to this new situation, he shared it with his brothers. James was first. As soon as he heard the news, he was infused with rush of eagerness. He felt strangely alert. Something new and momentous was taking place in their lives, under their very eyes, and they each had a central part to play. He placed his hand where Sam directed, and for the first time detected that unique movement that belongs only to childbirth. He felt transported into another realm, and his mind flooded with images of taking this child and teaching him the crafts of survival. He had no thought but that this would be a male child.

Alec had been waiting patiently, watching James' reaction. He knew that when Sam guided his hand to Molly's belly, he would not experience the same innocence of discovery. He had been alone with their mother when their brother Nathan had tried to come into the world, and he knew this process only through the memory of death. Determinedly he pushed that memory to one side, and for a while thought only of the gladness they were sharing, and the happiness that would come when they first heard the cry of the child. He placed his hand on Molly as Sam directed. Relief spread through him as he sensed the vitality beneath. Their mother had been exhausted, and she and Nathan had had no reserves with which to cope with their struggles. Molly's body radiated vibrant energy, and although each of his brothers moved but little, he felt the intensity of their collaboration. This birth could only go well.

Molly found that for a long time there was no pain, but as the hours passed, discomfort came, and then the pains. Her mind flooded with memories of her childhood, watching quietly while her mother attended women in such a situation. She was now greatly glad of this, because although it could never have prepared her fully for what her own body was undergoing now, she found that she remembered much of what her mother had done to help those women.

To begin with, there was time to rest between the pains, but gradually that time lessened, and the pain began to dominate her every moment. Whenever it faded, it seemed that there was no time before another began. When it overcame her, she lay on Alec's mattress. She took Sam's hand in hers, and showed him how to aid her bearing down, for when she was ready to push their baby out.

Alec fetched clean sacking. He had boiled it some weeks earlier, and had stored it ready in the baby's basket. He spread it across the lower part of his mattress, and waited quietly as the time drew nearer and nearer when the child would appear from between Molly's thighs.

The four did not have much longer to wait. Molly now looked as if she expected her body to divide into two parts, one part breaking away from inside her, and the other being left to recover. This in fact was true, but living out this experience together was quite different from merely carrying the taught knowledge. Molly's energies would be consumed totally by this final act, and the three brothers would witness and assist. Sam held the top of her belly, and applied gentle downward pressure when Molly directed. James held her hand, and Alec watched as the top of the baby's head appeared, receded, and then appeared again.

Then the baby's head was out, and Alec held it gently, drawing it to him as its body slipped away from Molly. Swiftly he cleaned its face with his hand, and it drew in a gasp of air and began to cry.

Sam cried out triumphantly 'My son!' and then leaned down to bite through the cord with his strong teeth.

Tenderly, Alec swaddled the boy in a blanket that Molly had knitted in readiness, and handed him to Sam, who placed him at Molly's breast. Then Alec backed away, and watched as James attended to the afterbirth. He was glad to be relieved of this duty, as it reminded him too strongly of his sad memory of Nathan's death. Although their own mother had then died too, they had nursed Molly back from the dead on this very mattress, and now she had borne a live baby that was a son for Sam, and a nephew for him and James. Yet he felt far more closely related to this child than as brother to the father. He longed to name this status, but there was no word to measuring the growth of the icy fingers, and each day he would check their size and make an announcement. James and Sam thought this to be greatly amusing, and they would fall about laughing at his news, but Molly was almost as interested as he. It was as if their pleasure and excitement about Nathan's progress could be extended to inanimate things.

Every fragment of dormant or shrivelled vegetation was fringed with frost, and the hens huddled together for warmth, their feathers fluffed out. The brothers kept the fire going day and night, and the stone chimney absorbed heat, radiating it out again to keep them warm.

The summer birds had departed long before Nathan's birth, leaving behind only those that could endure these hardships. When she had time, Molly loved to watch them through the small windows by drawing the skin covers to one side for a few minutes. She would save handfuls of chaff to toss to them, and then observe their busy search for morsels of nourishment. Small red-breasted ones were nearly always amongst those that would gather, ready in case her laden hand should appear, and she fancied that a friendship formed between them and herself.

The snows came again, but never with the same severity that had entrapped them at the crucial time. Each fall added to the last, but in between there was always opportunity to dig away enough to keep open the track to the village.

The pattern of darkness began to shift, allowing extra minutes of daylight. There were still many weeks of freezing hardship and long nights to endure, but the brothers began to turn their minds to the month of March, talking of their return to the Master's employ. Keen though they were to progress their plans, they never strayed from intent observation of every minute sign of Nathan's progress. He had begun to crow and gurgle happily, and the brothers passed multitudes of happy moments, conversing with him by mimicking his sounds.

Molly had continued to hum to Nathan. Sam had informed his brothers of this change in her, but as yet they had not heard it. She made the sound solely when absorbed in her care of Nathan, and when Alec and James were not there.

But then the day came when Alec was sitting quietly in the corner of the room, and he too heard it. He could not tell whether Molly was aware of his presence, or if she thought that she was alone. Sam was outside with James, clearing snow away from the side of the cottage where the wind had stacked it. From his mother's arms, Nathan lay awake and still, as if mesmerised by the beautiful sound, and Alec found himself slipping into a deeply peaceful state. After a while, Nathan's eyes closed, and Alec, too, fell asleep.

It was this scene that greeted Sam and James when they re-entered the cottage. James was the first to see Alec, and he nudged Sam, putting a finger to his lips, and pointing to his sleeping brother. Sam felt an urgent need to laugh. He spluttered, and hastily retreated back outside.

James was not thus affected. He stood quietly for a moment, and then said, smiling, 'Molly, I see you have woven a magic upon my brother and our nephew. Will you let me hear that magic?'

Molly smiled back to him, took a small breath, and continued to make her humming sound.

'What a sweet, sweet sound,' James whispered. 'Sam told us of it, but now you have let us hear it too. This is indeed a precious gift.'

Alec began to stir. As soon as he saw James, he said excitedly, 'I heard Molly's music.' Then he realised by the expression on his brother's face that he also had heard it.

It was then that, having quietened himself, Sam returned. Straight away he realised what had taken place, and he went to Molly, putting his arm round her shoulders. She looked up at him, touched her throat, and made more of the gentle humming sounds, before taking Nathan to his basket, and busying herself with some sewing.

Sam, James and Alec wanted to talk excitedly amongst themselves about the significance of what had just taken place, but they contented themselves with remarking upon the loveliness of Molly's voice. Although she concentrated upon her stitching, at times she glanced at them and smiled.

This new situation did not fade. Molly did not draw back into herself, and this progress never ceased to delight the brothers. When working outside, there were times when each of them would contrive to return, solely for the purpose of hearing Molly's voice thus engaged. Having waited the long months of more than a year, they never tired of it.

Yet the black hatred that the brothers carried became almost harder to bear. Now that Molly had this power, it made the absence of her speech all the more stark and agonising, and almost every day they would talk outside of their revenge. Waiting for March to come was both a longing for the new season and all the gifts it would bring, and brothers rose early, anticipating the challenge of the day with renewed energy. They crossed the moor at speed, arriving at Betty's house in good time. Even then, she was sitting on a stool at the gate, watching out for them. She greeted them all, then waved Alec and James on, thus ensuring Sam's attention before he left Molly. Boldly she put her plan to him.

Molly's eyes lit up instantly, and it took only that observation and the sight of her pleading gaze upon him for Sam to feel the urge to agree. However, he proceeded with caution, first asking what Liza would require in exchange for the use of her accommodation and her services. Betty was impressed by Sam's approach, and reassured him that nothing would be required, except the provision of their own food, and a portion of Molly's wage.

There was a twinkle in Betty's eyes as she said, 'At this very moment Liza awaits Nathan's arrival. Take him there now, and see for yourself. I promise that he will soon grow accustomed to her ways. Molly can walk to feed him later this morning, and also in the afternoon.'

Sam looked bemused, but Molly urged him with confident gestures. She kissed both Nathan and Sam, and he strode off, taking Nathan to Liza's dwelling. She must have been watching out for them, as she opened the door before he knocked. Then he could see with his own eyes the truth of Betty's promise, because when Liza took Nathan to her bosom, he remained calm as if he had already known this place. Before he left, Liza showed Sam a basket that she and Betty had woven together on long nights of that winter. They had filled it with the heads of cotton grass that she had collected from the moor after she had first considered Betty's proposal, and they had boiled layers of sacking to place upon the fresh white wadding.

Sam went to join Alec and Thomas with a spring in his step. He had been troubled by the possibility of harsh weather in the weeks of March, and the effect that this could have on Molly's ability to cross the moor with Nathan. His fears had been allayed as a result of Betty's careful planning, and he was greatly relieved. He greeted Thomas with enthusiasm, and discovered that the Master had sent word with him of the next building work that they were to undertake. The roof of a barn had collapsed under the weight of the winter snow, and was in urgent need of repair. This task had to be completed before embarking on the construction of a second row of cottages.

It struck Sam that Thomas was very familiar with the Master's affairs, more so than if he were acting as a particularly well-informed messenger, and he asked him how he had passed the last months. Thomas quietly informed him that he had been helping at the Master's house in various capacities, but Sam was left with a barely-tangible feeling that there was something about this that he was not being told. He decided that it was none of his business, and that if he were to know, he would find out without effort, so he did not press Thomas further. Instead, he asked him to lead them to the barn.

An initial inspection revealed that there was much to be done. The entire roof would need to be replaced, and the walls were in danger of collapsing. Sam immediately advised the construction of timbers to shore up the walls, followed by the building of buttresses. Once the walls were secured, then they could begin work on the roof.

'These repairs could take several months to complete,' he told Thomas.

'That was the Master's belief,' Thomas replied, 'but he wanted your opinion.'

Again Sam had the strange feeling. The way that Thomas had spoken surely indicated that he knew the Master better than could be accounted for by his station. Again Sam did not question Thomas further, and went to find Alec, who was surveying the smashed remains of the roof timbers.

'There is nothing here that we can use,' he observed regretfully. 'There is good timber here, but it will have to be used for smaller projects.'

'We can store it inside the finished cottages, and use it in the next row,' Sam decided. 'I will send word to the Master about this.'

'I will carry your decisions and requests to him,' said Thomas. 'I am his faithful messenger.'

There was now no longer any doubt in Sam's mind. Thomas' status with the Master was entirely beyond that of any ordinary worker. And Thomas' attitude in relation to Sam himself had changed. No longer was he a man who said but little, speaking only when spoken to. Instead he was of equal stature in conversation. This was a change that Sam found pleasing, and he welcomed the future effects of Thomas' new involvement. No doubt he would eventually learn why the change had come about, but for now it was sufficient to know it.

James came to find them in the early afternoon. He was eager to tell wagon. After that he checked the load regularly, contriving to be within earshot as much as possible.

He was rewarded for his diligence quite soon. The comment that had been passed at the barn, and the subsequent return of the men to the familiarity of the quarry, had loosened their tongues.

'When Mrs Lark first came to the village, at sixteen years of age we were grown, and knew the ways of the world,' said one.

The other grinned with an amiable expression on his face. 'No one knew what was under her apron, but we soon found out.'

'Miraculous she had done all that without a man,' the first commented with a twisted tongue.

The other sniggered quietly.

Neither man had halted his labour.

James was seething. They were speaking of Molly's beginnings with disrespect, and he wished that he could put a quick end to it. But not only could he not think of a way to do this without attracting unwelcome attention, but also he must learn whatever he could from their foul tongues.

The first man was speaking again. 'I listened out everywhere, but could glean no news of the baby's father.'

'I, too. It was of great intrigue to me at the time.'

'There were those who tried hard in conversation with Mrs Lark, but she would never be persuaded to let it slip.'

'Ha! She did not know,' said the other nastily.

'She knew all right,' replied the first. 'She just was not telling.'

'And all them good works,' said the other. 'Rescuing the fallen ones when their time came.'

Here the first corrected him firmly by saying, 'Hold your tongue. She treated all women with child the same.'

This last comment aided James in the task of restraining himself. He circled the cart, inspecting the stones as if to check the balance of the load.

The men never paused to take breath. Like the rest of the quarrymen, they were fit, and very strong.

The second continued, with a trace of a sneer in his voice. 'Sam's Nathan has had but one grandfather.'

It was then that the first confided, 'I heard a whisper of the other.'

The second almost stopped dead, but pushed himself on, lest he were reprimanded for slacking. 'What was it?'

'He was killed.'

'Killed? By what? And why did no one speak of it?'

The first dropped his voice very low, but James watched his lips. 'Killed by a man's hand. A blood relative.'

The other made as if the first had not spoken. He worked with greater speed, and soon moved round the other side of the cart. All his interest had evaporated so completely that it was as if he had never taken part in the conversation.

James' thoughts were churning. Why had he never heard this tale? He was certain that there had never been any mention of it. How had this man come by it? His muscles tensed painfully. He longed to get him on his own, and if necessary beat the details of the source from him. Silently he gave himself counsel to restrain himself, and to tell Sam and Alec the news at the earliest opportunity.

As soon as it was loaded, James left the quarry with that cart, arriving at the barn before noon. By great good fortune, Thomas and the two that had come this week from the quarry were working together to stabilise a wall, while Sam and Alec were making some final adjustments to roof timbers. James went straight to them, and squatted beside them as they worked.

'I heard it say that Molly's father was killed by the hand of a blood relative,' he reported starkly.

Sam dropped his tools to the ground and moaned. 'What mischief is this? Have we not had enough sorrow in our lives?'

Alec took his arm, and picking up the tools, placed them back in his hands. 'Work,' he instructed. 'No one must suspect the importance of the news.'

Sam instantly fell silent, and his body became as a machine, as his mind crowded with thoughts.

As a child he had never looked for Molly's father. To his young mind, her house had a man and a woman in it, and that had been sufficient. When he and Molly had married, the doctor had stood in the church in place of a father. He was recorded as a witness, and the father's name was written as 'unknown'. Sam had never minded this. In his heart, Molly had always been his, and that was what mattered. He had never heard tongues wagging about her parentage. He now realised that such tittle-tattle must have finished long before he was old enough to notice it. And now it seemed that with the birth of their son, some were questioning...

Sam had known Mrs Lark very well. She had been a hard-working and generous woman, who was always especially kind to children and the infirm. When he was a child it had seemed to him that he could go to her as if she were an extra mother, and he would run to see her if his own mother could not answer his questions. She was so knowledgeable that it seemed to him as if she knew everything. Now he could see that it was this that had led him to believe that she had told him everything she knew. But she had not! She must have known well who Molly's father was, and yet she had said nothing about him at all.

Sam had grown up knowing that there were women who had children without fathers. Such women were generally looked down upon. Those whose husbands had died of an illness were often believed not to have looked after them properly, whereas those whose husbands had died in an accident were treated with kindness. The rest were considered fallen women, but Mrs Lark had certainly managed to avoid that unwelcome status. Living in the doctor's house and becoming his assistant had given her a position that was above most of the other people in the village. She never used this to her advantage, and only employed it for the well-being of everyone she encountered.

Sam felt as if his heart were tearing in two. He had failed in his duty. He should have spoken to her about Molly's father. It had been his place as the prospective husband to do so. She must have thought that he did not want to know. Molly herself had never spoken of her father. Did she know who he had been, and what had happened to him? Why had he not asked her – if not before the wedding, afterwards, as he held her close to him, naked in bed? If she did know, she could not tell him now. She could not pass the knowledge to him by drawing in the ashes, and what other way was there for one who was mute?

Again Sam threw down his tools, and again Alec put them back in his hands, and ordered him to continue the task for which he was employed. Sam's mind raced on. Who else might know? Were there any that he could trust? Did Betty know? Did Liza know? Could he ask them? How could he ask them? He could see no way.

Then in his agony, Sam turned on his brothers and snarled, 'Why did you not know this before?'

Deeply affected by Sam's distraught state, James and Alec looked at each other accusingly. Then they shook their heads sadly, and James spoke for them both.

'We, like you, never knew the need. The question of Molly's parentage never came into our minds. Molly was always Mrs Lark's daughter, living at the doctor's house. No one ever referred to her differently.'

Alec spoke next. 'We have always loved her as if we were her brothers.'

'Aye,' James confirmed, 'ever since we ran together as children.'

Sam could see the truth of what his brothers were saying. For his part, he had never considered questioning their relationship with Molly after he had married her. Their relationship with her had never been any different, throughout the whole of their lives, and his marrying Molly had not changed that.

Alec continued. 'Right from when we were very young, James and I always knew that you would marry Molly, our sister.'

Sam looked at his brothers gratefully, and his heart was filled with sorrow that he had turned on them. 'Forgive me,' he murmured.

'There is nothing to forgive,' James told him.

'Aye,' said Alec stoutly. 'The pain of one is the pain of each.'

Sam rubbed his nose on the back of his hand before continuing quietly. 'There is much to be considered. If Molly's father was killed, we must find out by whose hand that was. It surely must throw light on who or what attacked her.'

'These were my thoughts as soon as I heard,' said James.

'We must act only after much deliberation,' Alec cautioned. 'There could still be possible danger to Molly and to ourselves.'

There was a grim note in Sam's voice when he announced, 'On Saturday, once we are home together, we will help Molly and Nathan to bed early, and we will make our plans.'

In the days until they would be home together again, Sam, Alec and James worked themselves harder in order to still their impatience and agitation. They spoke no more of what they had learned, and their few exchanges were only of the challenges of the repair of the barn.

At home together at nights, Alec and James barred the door carefully, and spoke little.

Then at last, the four were crossing the moor after work ended on Saturday, taking it in turns to carry Nathan. They passed comment freely to one another about what they had learned from Thomas about his position. Molly was greatly relieved to hear them speak thus. Her longing for them to know that he watched Mistress Mary for her safety had never gone away. Now that they knew this, it was as if her own life were more real. Of course, they were not to know of the suitor, or of the lovely clothing, but now they knew of Thomas' care of the Mistress, that was sufficient.

As Molly relaxed more deeply in their home, she appeared more tired than usual. Sam did not pay much heed to this, as it well suited his purpose. He put it down to Nathan's perpetual hunger, and Molly's being less accustomed to journeying across the moor.

Once Sam could see that Molly and Nathan were settled and sleeping, he added extra wood to the fire, and the brothers gathered round.

Sam spoke first. 'It has been on my mind to ask if you think the tale could be a cruel invention.'

James shook his head. 'If an invention were to be spread about, it would not be that.'

Alec nodded to indicate his agreement.

'We have to discover further sources of information,' said Sam, 'but it will not be easy.'

Alec stroked his beard. 'They must be trustworthy, and how are we to know that until we have the reaction to our enquiry?'

'The two men at the quarry worked as friends until the second knew. After that, he behaved as if they were strangers, or perhaps old enemies,' James reported.

'Perhaps the second plans to spread the story now,' Alec suggested.

'I doubt it,' James replied. 'He gave every impression of being filled with fear. It is my belief that he will behave as if he knows nothing.'

Sam contemplated this. 'There could be others like him.' He paused, and then asked suddenly, 'James, can you arrange that the man who told this tale comes back to the barn?'

'The two for next week are already picked,' James replied, 'but I can contrive that he returns here after that.'

'He should have with him someone who he might trust,' Sam said wisely. 'When he wearies of the lack of companionship at the barn, he may turn to him, and divulge the same, and more.'

Alec raised a question. 'Can we take Thomas into our confidence?'

'I wish 'twere so,' Sam replied. 'I have thought of it, but we must not.'

'Why not?' Alec pressed. 'If we did, he could work alongside the man who told the tale, and try to elicit more of it. As a protector of

Mistress Mary, he is well-practised in the art of quiet observation and astute questioning.'

'And he has already put certain trust in us,' James added.

Sam considered this. 'What should we say?'

'Tell him that we seek to establish more of Nathan's ancestry,' Alec advised. 'We could let him know that a mystery surrounds the absence of Molly's father, and that we do not want to upset her by asking openly. Make it plain that before Nathan's birth we three had no need to know, but now we must enquire on behalf of him.'

Sam savoured these words, and then pronounced, 'Brother, that sounds well, but we must first swear him to secrecy.'

James agreed with strength of purpose that was unmistakeable. 'That we must.'

'There is one more thing,' said Sam. 'It has been on my mind that Mrs Lark might have confided to Betty.'

Alec did not hesitate with his response. 'Brother, I think not.'

'There is no way to tell except by enquiry,' James replied.

'I agree with both of you,' said Sam. 'But let us think further about this if we cannot advance our search in the way we have planned.'

By surprising good fortune, one of the two quarrymen picked by James for Monday did not come to work. Instead he sent word by a neighbour that he had hurt his knee and could not walk. James took the opportunity to approach the man who had spoken of the death of Molly's father, to send him to the barn. The man did not object to this sudden change of plan. Instead he appeared quite pleased, and strode off immediately.

Meanwhile Alec had volunteered to run to the barn that morning, so that he would arrive well in advance of everyone else but Thomas, and could speak to him in private.

He arrived in good time, and he called to Thomas, who was sharpening one of his tools on a stone. Realising that this was about something important, Thomas left what he was doing, and engaged with Alec.

'Thomas, my brothers and I now have great trust in you,' Alec began, 'and I have come ahead today to tell you of a serious matter in which you may be able to assist us.'

'I will do what I can,' replied Thomas pleasantly.

Alec looked directly into Thomas' eyes, and said, 'First you must take a solemn oath never to reveal anything of this to others.'

'Such oaths have long been a part of my life,' Thomas assured him, 'and I have never failed to uphold any one of them.'

'Then swear.'

'I swear on pain of death that I will never reveal to any living soul anything of the matter about which you will speak.'

Alec acknowledged this oath by placing his left hand on Thomas' right shoulder, and then he spoke.

'Sam's son, Nathan, can never know his grandparents, as they have departed from this life, but we want to teach him their names. We knew three of them, but we know no one who knew the fourth. Will you help us in this search?'

'Aye, that I will,' Thomas promised.

'There is more. James overheard a quarryman tell of Molly's father being killed at the hands of a blood relative. We know that when Mrs Lark, Molly's mother, came to the village, she was with child, but of the father nothing was ever spoken. Soon James will have the quarryman come back here again to work. Will you labour alongside him, gain his confidence in daily matters, and report to us if he tells anything of the tale?'

'That I promise. One thing I must ask. Do you want me to lead him to the subject?'

'Only if he gives some particular sign. We do not want him to suspect that we have an interest.'

'You will already know that this is my skill. I will use it with precision.'

After this, the two men fell silent, and prepared for the day's labours.

Sam was not long in arriving.

'I have made the arrangement with Thomas,' Alec informed him quietly.

Sam looked pleased. He said nothing, but nodded to Alec and then to Thomas. A single quarryman joined them soon after this, and Alec asked him the whereabouts of the other.

'There was an accident in the village on Sunday. His knee is damaged,' he explained.

Alec put the quarryman to work, and turned back to his own task, but he had hardly begun to concentrate before he became aware of someone else approaching. He looked up and saw a figure moving quickly towards them.

This man soon came abreast of Sam and said, 'Your brother sent me in place of one with a bad knee. I am to tell you that he will be with us before noon.'

Sam acknowledged this message briskly. This man had been here before, and could be put to good use. But why would James be coming so soon? Then he had it! This was the very man whose mind they were pledged to examine.

'Thomas needs a strong man alongside him,' he said, pointing across to where he was hard at work.

The man grunted, and approached Thomas directly for instruction.

Well-satisfied with the direction events had taken, Sam absorbed himself in his tasks, looking forward eagerly to James' arrival.

The April sun had begun to warm the earth, and when rain came it was but soft and light, its presence interfering with nothing of what they were trying to accomplish.

About an hour later, Sam paused from his work, and saw James in the distance. He was striding along with the appearance of one who was intent upon great purpose. Sam returned his attention to his task. Although his every sense was directed towards his approaching brother, he did not want the quarryman to know that this was of particular importance to him.

When James came to his side, he looked up and said, 'Ho, brother! Your arrival is well-timed. I need a man to lift here, and did not want to draw on the others.'

James wrapped his arms around the beam that Sam had been preparing, and Sam smiled and continued. 'The men we needed here came swiftly, and they work well.' Then he said out of the corner of his mouth, 'I trust the second you sent is the one?'

On the surface, James appeared not have heard this, but he nodded as he threw all his strength into shifting the beam.

The addition of the extra men allowed greater progress that more than merited their presence, and Sam was confident that the Master would be well-pleased with the results of their request. When the quarrymen left for home, Sam, Alec, and James spoke to Thomas.

'How goes it?' asked Sam.

'The man is a good worker. He willingly does more than he need for his wages,' Thomas reported. He looked at James with a certain expression, and added, 'You have chosen well.' Then he turned and checked round the walls of the barn before returning to say, 'We spoke a little. I gave him news from the Master's house. It was nothing that is not already well-known here. He wanted more, but I left him with that hunger. He then told me a tale from the village, and I feigned interest for further detail. I think that when he returns tomorrow, each will have more to tell the other.'

At that, the brothers shook his hand, and then departed, Sam to collect Molly and go to Nathan, and Alec and James to return home.

Chapter Twenty

In the middle of the week, Molly arrived at Betty's to find her in a state of considerable excitement. Betty barely acknowledged Sam's presence before she hurried Molly inside. This in itself was very unusual, and Molly knew that something momentous must have happened. Sam stared at the closed door from the gate, smiled to himself good-naturedly, and strode off in the direction of the barn. Thomas had told of further progress with the quarryman, and he was eager to see what today would bring.

In the workroom, Molly had barely sat down before Betty began.

'We are to have a visit from Mistress Mary this very day!' she exclaimed, trying to keep her voice low, and not quite succeeding. She clapped her hands to her mouth. 'Mercy me!' she mumbled through her fingers, 'No one must overhear.' She took a deep breath and then said, 'A servant girl called last evening. She brought a gift of ducks' eggs for us from the Master's kitchens. Of course, it was a subterfuge, but a greatly generous one. The girl gave me the message that the Mistress would call at noon today, and would be the bearer of much news. Molly, you must run to feed Nathan in good time, so that you return well before her arrival.'

As Molly listened, she felt increasing excitement rising like the flight of a bird inside her. She loved tending the Mistress, albeit secretly, and she was eager for news of the suitor. Would they learn more that day? Where was he from? Who could he be? Was he truly worthy of her hand? That last question was the most prominent in her mind. Every day she knew well the precious bond that joined her to Sam, and she wanted the Mistress to know the same with a husband. The Mistress had good relations with her brother, that was clear, and she had Thomas as her devoted protector. This meant that she must be cared for much as Alec and James cared for herself. That was indeed good. What she and Betty had heard already about the suitor boded well. For a moment she wished that Mistress Mary and the Master could have had such a good woman as her own mother, but it had not been the case, and that time was gone.

As they stitched, Betty could not stop talking. She tried her best to quiet herself, but she was like some birds that Molly had observed. She twittered, and her twittering was without end, rising and then falling, but never ceasing. There were many occasions when Molly had to put a finger to her lips to warn her of the loudness of her excited utterances. Much of what she said was exactly what was in Molly's own mind, unspoken, and Molly found it easy to listen to her.

True to her word, Betty sent Molly early to feed Nathan. And as Molly ran to Liza's cottage, she wondered if, despite her absence, Betty were still twittering.

When she returned, Betty instructed her to wipe the stools clean, and place them outside the entrance door again. They had been in the kitchen all winter, but by good fortune, today was bright, and the noon sun would be just warm enough for sitting a while. She had saved a good amount of her best camomile right through the winter for such an eventuality.

All was ready, and now they must wait. Every few minutes, Betty sent Molly to the door to see if the Mistress was approaching. She had gleaned that Mistress Mary was of a punctual nature, but she could not put aside the possibility that she might arrive early, and she did not wish to be surprised thus. Her heart jolted pleasantly when Molly came dashing from the door after the fourth investigation. They put down their sewing, and while they waited for the sound of the knocking, Betty carefully flexed her knees in preparation to receive the Mistress, as she did not want her stiffness to be apparent.

The Mistress smiled when Betty opened the door. It was a warm, kindly smile. 'You need not bend,' she instructed, 'but a cup of your best camomile would be most welcome.'

Betty called to Molly to fetch it, while she settled the Mistress on the better of the two stools.

'The sun is quite warm, is it not?' Mistress Mary commented pleasantly, and then in a low voice added, 'I have much to tell.'

Betty heard Molly in the passageway. She took the cup from her, and passed it to the Mistress.

'Could you ask Molly to stand at the gate?' the Mistress requested. 'It would be most agreeable to watch her enjoying the air.'

Knowing exactly what Mistress Mary intended, Betty took Molly to the gate, and told her to report instantly anything that might cause disturbance. Then she sat on the other stool.

'Draw a little closer, Betty,' the Mistress told her between sips.

Betty did this. Out of the pocket of her apron she produced a small piece of cloth and some coloured threads, and with deft use of her needle she concentrated her attention upon creating a flower.

'Betty, your resourcefulness is to be greatly admired,' said the Mistress. Then she took another sip before confiding. 'There are cousins by my mother's sisters. I have heard that they surely wish me ill, and they seek to find ways to discredit me. I cannot risk them learning of my suitor.'

Betty glanced at her, and could see that her face had turned quite pale. She reached for the cup, offering to refill it.

The Mistress shook her head. The cup was empty, but she said in a clear voice, 'I have plenty here.'

Betty understood the message straight away, and she watched Molly intently for any change in her posture.

The Mistress continued. 'May is a month full of blossoming, and it is the anniversary of my mother's death. I had hoped for more freedom, and my beloved had intended to declare our betrothal in June. Yet now this cannot be. I cannot risk it.'

Here Betty noted that Mistress Mary's demeanour became more that of a girl as she turned to Betty and begged in a forced whisper, 'Betty, will you quickly make me some beautiful garments from grey material? After the anniversary of my mother's death, no one can fault that colour.' She added with quiet passion, 'I long for brightness, and I oft wear the ruby-red and the emerald-green in the privacy of my room.' Then she seemed to realise that she had cast her womanly dignity to one side, and sipped from her long-empty cup.

Molly thought that she could detect some agitation in the posture of Mistress Mary's servant companion who stood a little distance away. Then she herself heard something. She turned, glanced towards Betty, and then looked towards the side of the cottage from which the noise had come. The air was still, and yet she detected movement in the thorny thicket. Although grown for a windbreak, it could also conceal unwanted attentions, and she was sure that she spied a dark shape moving behind the dense, leafless branches.

Betty laid her sewing on her knee and declared loudly, 'I sense a chill in the air. I will fetch you an extra shawl directly.'

When she returned with the shawl, the Mistress had regained her composure. She drew herself up, and said in a voice that would allow anyone nearby to overhear, 'Betty, I have acquired some serviceable grey cloth. It is of a slightly paler hue than I had sought.' Here she lowered her voice to an almost inaudible murmur. 'And I fancy I can sometimes perceive a tinge of duck-egg blue in it.' Then she took time to sip meditatively from her empty cup. After that she projected her voice a little, adding, 'I am sure my dear mother herself would approve the cloth, and had she still been alive, she would have aided me kindly in the selection of it. I will arrange that it is delivered to your door this very afternoon.' At that, she passed her cup to Betty, and stood up. Then she rearranged her skirts, and made towards the gate. Molly quickly lowered her head and stood to one side as she passed.

Back in the privacy of the workroom, Betty said, 'You did well, Molly. You detected something, did you not?'

Molly nodded her head vigorously.

'The Mistress' secrets are safe with us.' Betty sighed. 'I wish that her trusty watchman, Thomas, could be with her at all times, but that would draw unwanted attention to his presence in these parts. It is indeed better that he is a worker, keeping his eyes and ears open, and reporting all signs to the Master. Molly, as soon as the grey cloth is brought here, we must put aside everything else and work long hours to complete the first dress. I will speak to Liza to enquire whether or not she can offer you lodgings for the month of May.'

Molly had been listening intently to everything that Betty was saying, and she agreed with every word of it. She knew that Liza would fall in immediately with any suggestion of her spending the weeks of May there. In fact, she had already begun to hint this to Sam. Molly missed her own home, but her wish to be here was even greater. She wanted to be fully involved in this intrigue, and she wanted Mistress Mary's life to take a turn in the direction that she deserved. Yet even more than this, Molly longed passionately for the return of her voice. She knew that at some time in the future she would spend more of her hours in her own home. She believed that with time and perseverance, and with the help of faithful supporters, Mistress Mary could marry her suitor. Yet she had no conception of how she could reclaim her voice. She had been so glad when the others had helped her to see that she was humming to Nathan, and since that time, she had never lost that awareness, but beyond that she had not progressed.

As Betty spoke to Molly, she was all too painfully aware of Molly's sorely limited ability to have conversation. Betty was hungry for interaction. They shared a secret, and could only trust each other with it. Thus, Betty had no one else to speak to. Mistress Mary's visits were infrequent, and the dialogue that they had was constrained by Betty's station and by the urgent need for caution. Then a thought struck her. Perhaps the Mistress herself longed for the freedom to exchange thoughts, ideas and emotions about her situation, but had no one in whom she could confide more than in these brief encounters at Betty's door. Their interaction there was potent, but stilted, and by the nature of their positions, Betty was not free to respond in any way other than as a kind of ritual. Yes, she could convey a deeper message through this, but never with words. Although Betty had a voice, she must barely use it in this respect. This meant that her position regarding the Mistress had similarities to Molly's lack of conversation. Thus comforted, Betty began to consider what this must be like for Molly. Before, she had thought only of how to restore Molly's voice, and had not considered enough how she must be feeling without it. This was not surprising, because Molly had made no sign of being distressed by the absence of it. In fact, until she had begun to hum to Nathan, it had been the opposite, as she had clearly been greatly distressed by the fragments of its presence. Betty thought again of the peg dolls, and of her spell. It was very obvious to her that they had contributed to Molly's improvement, but maybe there was something more that she should add before further progress could be made. Betty resolved to contemplate this.

But before she could concentrate her thoughts upon this matter, there was a knock at the door.

'Mercy me!' she exclaimed. 'Run quickly, Molly.'

Molly jumped up and ran to the door. There she found two servants each bearing a sack. 'For Mistress Mary's dress order,' said one.

Molly stood to one side while they pushed them in. Then saying nothing else, they turned and left. Molly dragged the sacks to the workroom, and stacked them by the wall.

'Run and feed Nathan directly,' Betty ordered. Then she stopped and changed her mind. 'Nay, we should inspect the content of these before you go.'

A smile spread across Molly's face. Much as she wanted to spend her precious minutes with her son, equally she wanted a glimpse of this cloth before she ran to him.

Betty loosened the mouth of the first sack, and tugged at a corner of the material, revealing a creation that bore a wondrous sheen.

Molly felt air surging into her lungs, and she gasped loudly.

Betty did not know whether to cling to the cloth or to Molly. In one strange thought, she saw an image of herself holding Molly, whom she had wrapped in it. A shout of joy escaped from Molly's lips, closely followed by her hand flying to her mouth to silence it.

Betty was overcome, but she quickly steadied herself and whispered, 'Molly 'tis surely the most beautiful colour I have ever beheld. An' 'tis so gentle to the touch.' She moved to one side so that Molly could take her place.

As Molly handled the material, a look came into her eyes that reminded Betty of the kind of mists that sometimes rose from the moor – the rare ones that augured good fortune.

Some minutes passed, and then Betty asked carefully, 'Did you hear the gasp that escaped your lips?'

Molly smiled and nodded. She had certainly heard it, and it had pleased her. She was glad that Betty had heard it too.

Betty hugged her, and then said, 'Run and feed Nathan, and return here directly.'

Molly needed no second bidding. She ran as fast as she could to Liza's cottage, waiting for a moment to catch her breath before entering. Nathan had his back to the door, as he was engaged in a happy game with Liza, who had him on her knee and was helping him to use his chubby fingers to press on her nose. He was chuckling delightedly, and at first did not notice his mother's presence. Then he turned, and when he saw her, he put out his arms with the unformed shout of an infant.

Again Molly sucked air into her lungs, and heard herself gasp.

Liza was so astonished that she almost let Nathan wriggle out of her arms. She steadied him just in time, before he slipped off her knee and onto the hardened earth at her feet.

Molly knelt beside Liza and put her arms round Nathan, taking him to her joyfully. When finished, he fell asleep, and Molly placed him tenderly in the basket, before running back to start work on the first grey dress.

'I have a plan,' Betty confided as they began to measure and cut. 'We shall use some of what remains of the black to make a fine shawl, and several good aprons for the Mistress to wear over her grey dress. The shawl will be made of two black layers, sewn together and decorated with black threads. That way none can challenge her. Her manner of dress will state without doubt her continuing intention to honour her mother's death.'

So pleased was she with Betty's plan that Molly clutched her hand and gave a little shudder of delight.

When Sam arrived at the end of that afternoon, Molly lingered at the door, waiting for Betty to join them. As the three stood together, she placed a hand at her throat, and drew in her breath in an audible gasp. Betty watched as Sam's face radiated joy and happiness. She waved goodbye to them at the gate, as hand in hand they walked to see Liza and Nathan.

Perhaps, thought Betty, I will not yet need to conceive how to add strength the spell.

Chapter Twenty-one

With every day that passed that week, Thomas edged his way further and further into the quarryman's confidence. Alec, James and Sam arranged that Thomas took tasks that ensured many hours of close proximity with the man, and they made no further move to question Thomas about his researches until the week was past.

The two quarrymen departed together at the end of the afternoon that Saturday, and when the others were sure that they were out of sight, they sat together on a heap of stones where they could see the approach of a person from any direction.

'I am greatly perplexed,' Thomas told them. 'There are many parts to this, and as yet I cannot understand it.'

'Tell us all you know,' Sam requested.

Thomas began.

'As you know, I found it simple to exchange news of no consequence, as the man has a great propensity for such chatter. Such was the sense of ease that was quickly established between us, before long the man asked me directly if I knew of Nathan's ancestry. I told him that I had been in these parts for less than a year, and knew nothing of it. This unleashed the results of considerable deliberation on his part, as if it had been preying on his mind. I think that he had found no talking companion for this subject, the last having backed away from him with determination.'

'That is what I observed,' James confirmed.

Thomas continued. 'He is entirely certain that Molly's father was killed before she was born. He is also sure that he died at the hands of a blood relative.'

'How can he be certain?' asked Sam.

'A distant relation of his on his mother's side happened to live in the village where the death took place.'

'But if that is the case, he must have known all this before,' said James. His voice was harsh. 'So why would this exercise his mind now?'

'The birth of Nathan is the most likely cause,' Alec pointed out.

'Nathan's birth only added to the tale,' said Thomas. 'It was not the centre of it.'

'Then what is?' asked Sam.

'The village where the death took place is far away. Mrs Lark was never known there, but Molly's father knew it well. He had travelled there that day.'

'For what reason?' Sam questioned.

'I know not. All I know is that he met his end, and never again returned to Mrs Lark.' Thomas paused, as if to gather himself, before saying, 'Rumour had it that it was his own father who killed him.'

Sam cried out in anguish. 'Molly's grandfather, a murderer! That cannot be.'

'I cannot vouch for the truth of it,' Thomas reminded him.

Sam was beside himself. 'The hands of the murderer. Tell me about the hands of the murderer,' he pressed urgently.

'I know nothing of them,' Thomas replied.

Alec tried to calm him. 'Hush, Sam. Thomas knows no more.'

James put an arm round Sam's shoulder in an attempt to steady him. But instead his action achieved the opposite effect.

Sam flung his arm away, and glared at Thomas, roaring, 'I must know about the hands!'

Alec was alarmed. 'Sam, Thomas knows no more, but he will help all he can.'

Thomas looked straight into Sam's eyes. 'That I promise. But Sam, there is more you want to say.'

At this Sam quietened. 'Aye, there is more we must tell you now.'

'Shall I speak?' James asked Sam.

'Nay, 'tis for me to say.' Sam gathered himself, and then began. 'A year ago in December, we brothers were returning to our cottage with some rabbits. We found our dear Molly had been left for dead on the floor with a great gash in her head, and ugly bruises round her neck and shoulders. We nursed her back to life, but since that day, she has spoken fewer words than I can count with one hand. For a long time, we spoke nothing to her of the attack, but then she showed me she wanted to know what had happened to her voice. I believe that since we told her of how we found her and nursed her she has remembered something of the attack, but she cannot tell us.'

'I knew of your Molly's affliction,' said Thomas, 'but I did not enquire as to its origin. Amongst the servants at the Master's house, there is much sympathy for her.'

Sam was greatly reassured to hear this, and some of the tension in his body began to drain away. Kind thoughts would certainly help Molly, and in addition it was comforting for him that it seemed Betty had never spoken to a soul of what little she knew from James when she had given him honey for Molly.

He continued. 'Thomas, the hands that caused her injury were of a size that I have never known.' He took one of James' hands. 'See how this exceeds the size of my own. The marks on Molly were from hands far greater.'

Even though he was accustomed to violent tales, Thomas felt strangely burdened by the horror of this knowledge.

Sam's voice was quiet when he asked, 'Thomas, can you aid us in finding a way of discovering more? I want to know more of her grandfather. If 'tis true that he killed his own son, then surely he was mad.'

'My employment is with Mistress Mary's suitor,' Thomas reminded him. 'I cannot journey from this place, and I fear that learning about Molly's grandfather could mean travel of many days.'

Sam persisted. 'But will you tell us of anything you hear.'

'You have already taken me into your confidence, and I am under oath never to reveal any of this. I pledge to tell you all that is of note.'

'Are you willing to speak again to that quarryman?' asked James.

'I cannot see how,' Thomas replied. 'He has already had his time here, and more. Before he can come again, there are many who must take his place.'

Although James knew that this was true, he wrestled with it. 'I could devise a way for him to return,' he began.

Thomas shook his head. 'There is no good reason, and he will know that. It will raise suspicions in him, and we cannot take that risk.'

Sam kicked at a stone angrily. He felt defeated.

'Have faith, brother,' Alec counselled. 'The information about Molly's father was unexpected, and it came to us by chance. If we are patient, more may come, and in ways that we cannot predict.'

Sam looked at him. 'I have waited long enough,' he stated coldly. Then fixing his mind on seeing Molly and Nathan again, he walked quickly away from them.

James made as if to follow, but Alec took him by the arm. 'Stay,' he advised. 'Let him go now. We will speak to him again tonight.' Then he said to Thomas, 'Many thanks, trusted friend. May your

Mistress remain safe in your care. We will see you after Sunday is gone.'

Sam sped to Liza's cottage, where she was waiting for him with Nathan sleeping in her arms. He took him gently, and bade her goodbye. Close to his son, he felt his heart ease. It took him little time to reach Betty's house, and he knocked gently on the door so as not to wake him. Molly appeared soon after, and together they crossed the moor in the twilight.

When they came in sight of their dwelling, Nathan woke, and he spent the rest of the journey sucking at his father's ear. They arrived home to find that James and Alec had lit the fire, and were making broth. Molly sat down to feed Nathan, who took from her hungrily, and was then wakeful all evening, eager to play. This provided a welcome diversion for the brothers, each of whom had been burdened with their circling thoughts of what they had learned from Thomas that day. They devised a game of passing Nathan between them, making first as if to throw him. He screamed and crowed with delight, reaching out his arms as each brother caught him.

Molly took Nathan to their room, and hummed while he fell asleep. Filled with the pleasure of their evening's play, the brothers were relaxed in one another's company, and instead of returning to the terse interaction that they had begun at the barn, they took to jesting. From her place by Nathan's side, Molly listened to them. It was a comfort to her to hear their jollity, and she drifted into slumber.

Sunday was a day spent in preparing the enclosure further for the hoped-for calf, and breaking ground ready for seeds. The brothers strengthened parts of the surrounding wall. Easter was late in coming this year, but they would soon learn whether or not the Master had a calf for them.

The day was bright, and while Nathan was sleeping, Molly took some clothing to the stream, and made it clean in the clear waters, afterwards spreading it on the wall of the enclosure. Perhaps when Mistress Mary next came to Betty's house, they would learn something of the mysterious suitor. Molly hugged this question to herself as she went about her tasks. Working on the grey material gave her a feeling of anticipation. She had no doubt that this feeling was shared by Betty, who exclaimed regularly, but in a low voice, about the quality of the cloth and the future prospects of the Mistress.

When evening came, Sam approached Molly, asking her to leave him alone with Alec and James. At first she felt perturbed. He had not asked anything like this before. Then she saw the look in his eyes, and she trusted that whatever the reason for his request, there was rightness in his intention.

Once Molly was settled, Sam turned to the others. 'The news has tried me sorely.' He clenched his fists until his knuckles turned white. 'I want to pin down the man at the quarry, and force him to tell me all that he knows.'

'I do not know if I can go to the quarry tomorrow,' James confessed. 'I may not be able to hold back.'

'I have similar thoughts,' Alec told them, 'but I know that beating it out of him might yield less than more subtle means.'

Sam and James stared at him.

Alec explained. 'He may know more than he realises. We must help him to bring it out where we can see it.'

'You are as a cunning fox,' Sam observed. 'How do you propose that we stalk and corner him?'

'We must endeavour to shadow him, and remember, what we are stalking is his thoughts and memories. Cornering him might not elicit what we want.'

'I have long thought of visiting the village,' James confided. 'I think that time is nigh. Next month the evenings are longer, and this will afford the time. Until then I will watch him closely at the quarry. He may let something out. He likes me well enough, but I must take care not to spend too much time in his company.'

After this, Sam fell silent.

Then Alec asked, 'What is in your mind?'

'I want to know the name of the place,' he replied. 'I want to know where Molly's father breathed his last.'

'To what end?' Alec enquired.

'I want to find the exact spot,' Sam answered with grim determination etched on his brow.

'We have been told the journey there is long,' James pointed out. 'It could be over a day's walk away. How then could you return in time for work?'

'And Molly would be without you,' Alec added.

'I would walk through the night, and carry her with me in my heart,' said Sam stubbornly.

James realised that Sam had made up his mind, and he began to fear for his safety. 'You must promise me that you will do nothing until we have more news of the location,' he begged. 'The value of your journey will be nothing without that,' he added bluntly.

Alec narrowed his eyes and spoke brutally. 'Sam, Molly will be bereft without you. And what of Nathan?'

This seemed to penetrate Sam's blindness, and he moaned. ''Tis too hard to do nothing.'

'You perceive wrongly,' Alec corrected him. 'We have much to do every day, but we must give no sign of it.'

Sam sighed. 'You are right. We conceal our actions so well that there are many times when they are invisible, even to those who know them.' Then he addressed both James and Alec. 'Brothers, if I again stray in my thinking, remind me of this night, lest I endanger myself or others.'

Chapter Twenty-two

Monday brought with it much that was new. When James arrived at the quarry, the very man approached him straight away, asking to work at the barn again.

'I cannot arrange that,' James replied firmly, while longing to send him immediately.

'One whose time it is this week cannot walk well,' said the man. 'His ankle is twisted. He will arrive soon, and can help with the repair of the carts, but he cannot walk any further.'

Just then, James saw the man making his way slowly up the track, leaning heavily on a staff.

James hesitated. Would this arrangement cause trouble amongst the men? He walked briskly to meet the injured man.

When he came to him he asked, 'Can you walk to the barn today?'

'Nay, that I cannot do. I can bide here and help with many things, but I can walk no further.'

His mind made up, James decided to send their prey to the barn. 'Ho!' he cried. 'Make haste to the barn, and be there for this day. Tell Alec that I sent you.'

The man set off, and James watched the quarrymen closely for any sign of envy that would disturb their labours. But there was no such unrest. In fact, the men seemed happy with his decision, and he overheard one or two of them expressing that they were glad not to have been sent.

At noon he left word with the man with the injured ankle that the arrangement would remain the same the following day, and he made his way to the barn.

Betty and Molly were taken by surprise when they heard a knock at the door. Betty dropped her sewing, and threw up her hands.

'I am not expecting a caller,' she said nervously. She passed her stitching to Molly and hauled herself to her feet, making her way to the door as quickly as she could.

Molly heard her voice as she opened the door. 'Why, Mistress

Mary…' Betty had been taken completely by surprise, and she felt entirely uncertain about what to do.

'Good morrow, Betty.' The Mistress spoke as if Betty had said nothing. She held herself confidently, but Betty could see that she looked flustered.

A servant was standing at the gate, looking away from the house.

'I have a problem with the hem of my dress,' the Mistress announced, in a voice that seemed louder than necessary. 'I caught my toe in it this very day. I trust you can repair it if I come in.'

'Of course, Mistress Mary. That I can,' Betty replied, picking up the hint with alacrity.

Betty let the Mistress pass her in the corridor, and directed her to the kitchen, where she gave her a seat at the table.

'I will fetch Molly,' she said as she backed out of the room.

'Molly, come quickly! The Mistress has need of our help,' she called.

Molly hurried to her, carrying needles and black thread. But when they entered the kitchen together, the Mistress lifted her skirts to reveal that there was no damage.

'Make a pretence of sewing the hem,' she instructed in a whisper. 'Betty, I must speak with you. I have a letter here for my suitor. I am being watched too closely at the house, and I fear discovery. I dared not send the letter, but I have sent word for a messenger to call here by dead of night to collect it.' Her cheeks flushed. 'My beloved lives some miles beyond the village. He will send one of his trusted horsemen.'

Just then, Molly felt certain that she had glimpsed a shadow at the window. Quickly, she dug her needle into Mistress Mary's leg.

'You clumsy girl!' the Mistress exclaimed angrily.

Affronted, Betty glared at Molly. How could she be so stupid?

Then the Mistress read the expression on Molly's face. She put a hand on Molly's and squeezed it. 'My gratitude,' she murmured.

There was much activity at the barn that day. The walls had been greatly strengthened. Weeks ago, thick hemp ropes had been employed to hoist and hold fast the heavy roof timbers. Now all was being secured to last for decades to come. The brothers had had no sight of the Master, but he had visited regularly at quiet times to inspect their progress, and had sent word by a servant of his satisfaction. The brothers had learned this very day secretly from

Thomas that the Master was indeed greatly impressed by the quality of their work, and was making plans to secure their services permanently. And a heifer calf would be theirs by the end of May. This news warmed their hearts, and added strength to their shoulders. Their future surely looked prosperous.

Yet inside Sam there was a dark place, cold as the very stone that they handled.

'The Mistress trusts us completely,' Betty repeated to Molly many times that day. Molly noticed that each time she said this she stitched faster than ever before. 'We have her confidence in all matters. She will surely use our services for as long as she lives. She is still but a young woman. I will be in her employment until I am old and able stitch no more. An' you, Molly, you have already learned nearly all I can show to you. There is no doubt that you will stitch far longer than I, and for many a long year the Mistress will send to you whenever she is in need, whether it be for her clothing or for a safe ear.' She dropped her sewing for a moment, and rubbed her hands together excitedly. 'The month of May is well-nigh here. Liza will speak to your Sam, an' you and Nathan will bide with her for those weeks, so we can finish this dress apace.'

Throughout this, Molly smiled and nodded. When Betty paused for breath, Molly reached into their bag of scraps, and pulled out a fragment of the black lace. Then she held it up, and pointed in turn to it and to herself.

'You want that scrap?' asked Betty. 'I think the Mistress would allow it.'

Molly shook her head emphatically, and this time pointed to the lace and then to her hands.

'Now I have it!' exclaimed Betty. ''Tis in your mind to learn how to make it yourself.'

Molly's face shone as she nodded so emphatically that Betty feared she would do her neck some harm.

'Have a care,' she advised kindly. 'I have your meaning already. We must think on this. I will speak to Liza.'

Everything was progressing better than Betty could have dreamed. The misfortunes of the Mistress had led her to place ever more trust in them, and through this she had discovered great comfort. In turn, Betty and Molly could now be quite certain of an income. Their loyalty to their Mistress and her cause was without question and would never falter.

Yet the subject of Molly's voice hung heavily upon Betty. It was still so sorely lacking, and even the recent improvement was very small, and rarely repeated.

Molly herself was greatly sustained by the communication that had taken place between herself and the Mistress that morning. She knew that she had taken a terrible risk when she had plunged her needle into Mistress Mary's leg, and yet she also knew that the risk would have been far greater had she not. In the look that they had shared, Molly had seen that her Mistress had understood it all. And because of it, Molly knew that they had the kind of bond that could never be broken.

When the day ended, Thomas signalled to Sam that he should linger on when the others departed. Sam had no difficulty in finding things to absorb his attention while the quarrymen prepared to leave. He even told Alec and James to get on their way, and he led them to believe that Molly and Liza were to take Nathan to see a neighbour, and would not be home until later. This meant that they did not question his slowness.

All was quiet, and Thomas and Sam found a safe spot, where they sat back to back on a rock, keeping watch.

'I have the name of the place,' Thomas told him.

'You have done well. Did he suspect anything?'

'He could have no suspicion. He said the name without any enquiry from me.'

'Tell me then.'

'First you must promise not to travel there alone.'

Sam sprang to his feet, grabbed Thomas by the front of his shirt, and began to shake him. Thomas did not resist. Instead, he looked straight into Sam's furious eyes.

Sam stopped, and released his grasp. He bowed his head, and knelt in front of Thomas.

'Nay,' said Thomas, 'get to your feet. This is not the way to be.' He reached out and shook Sam's hand.

At this Sam stood up and said, 'I give you my solemn pledge that I will not travel to that place alone.'

Thomas gazed carefully about them, and then said, ''Tis a place many hours' walk from here.'

'How many?' asked Sam.

Thomas looked at him sharply.

Lifting one eyebrow, Sam added, 'I give you my assurance that my question is no indication of a plan to leave by nightfall.'

Thomas' shoulders relaxed, but he said, 'My friend, you are in peril if you break your pledge.'

Sam inclined his head to acknowledge the seriousness of what Thomas had told him.

'The name of the place is Mortbridge. By road it takes most of a full day to reach it. Taking to the heath and hills, a good man who knows the way can arrive much sooner.'

'The name signifies that the people who lived there have known more than one death,' said Sam slowly. He sat down again on the rock, and put his chin in his hands. ''Twould be a sizeable undertaking.'

'And would require an experienced travelling companion.'

'One who can be trusted entirely. As yet I know not of such a person.'

'That is good,' said Thomas wisely. 'That way you will not be tempted to break your promise.'

'Soon it will be May,' Sam mused. 'James will idle away some of his Sunday in the village. He might gather in something of note.'

'Aye, that he may, and that would be a better way.'

'Thomas, did the quarryman tell you anything more of the murder?' asked Sam suddenly.

Although highly experienced in the art of intrigue and subterfuge, Thomas was taken by surprise. He had come to regard Sam as a trusted friend, and because of this, he had softened his guard. His eyes were not hooded, and Sam saw his answer there.

'Tell me now,' he said quietly.

Thomas shook his head. 'You must not know yet.'

Then a terrible rage came up inside Sam, and he thought in that instant that he would throw Thomas to the ground. Although Thomas saw this, he did not make ready to defend himself, and he did not flee. Instead he took his knife from his belt and made a nick in one finger, letting the blood drip onto the ground by Sam's feet.

Straight away Sam knew what this meant. Grimly, he took his own knife and did likewise. Then the two men put the bleeding fingers together, and let the blood mix.

'Brothers in blood, we are joined in the same purpose,' said Thomas. Then as he repeated it, Sam spoke it with him.

'I trust you to tell me everything when the time is right,' Sam told him, 'though the hunger for that knowledge eats at me every waking hour.'

'Well I know that,' replied Thomas. 'Yet I must wait, lest I speak before all is clear enough.'

This explanation allowed Sam enough peace to accept Thomas' decision. They said no more, and left by different tracks. Sam was glad that he would not see James and Alec that night, as he did not want to speak of what had just taken place.

That evening, Betty spoke to her husband of the expected arrival of the night traveller. He grunted in response, but Betty fed him well, and then showed him the place where she had concealed Mistress Mary's letter. Before she went to bed, she put on her best nightgown, and settled the farrier in his favourite chair to await the sound of horse's hooves.

It was not until the early hours of the morning that he heard a sound. He had been dozing, and at first wondered if that noise had been in a dream. He stiffened. There was certainly movement outside, but it was not the familiar thud of horses' hooves. Then he heard a hiss at the window, and he put the letter inside his jacket and hurried to the door. In the darkness he could just make out the figure of a boy.

'Mistress Mary's letter,' the boy whispered.

With some misgiving, the farrier reached inside his jacket. Then changing his mind, he grabbed the boy, and took him round the side of the house. There a cloaked horseman was waiting on a mare. To his great astonishment the farrier could see that the hooves of the mare were exceptionally large, being bound in swathes of sacking.

'My master is the suitor,' the rider confirmed.

The farrier passed the letter to the horseman, who secured it underneath his cloak. Then he reached down and took the boy's hand. The boy leaped up agilely behind him, and the mare moved away at a good speed but with very little sound.

The farrier scratched his head, perplexed. In all his life he had never seen the like of this. Then he put the scene out of his mind as he remembered the sight of Betty's best nightgown.

Chapter Twenty-three

Since the day of her dream, Molly had put little further thought into the remembered horrors. She had no wish to hold such things in her mind. She wanted to know only the happiness of being with Nathan and her menfolk, and of working with Betty for Mistress Mary. Any spare moments she had were to be filled with dreams of making lace. Since Betty had understood how passionately she felt about this, Molly was counting the days until Sunday, the day when she hoped that Betty might speak to Liza.

Yet despite all of this, there was a nagging at the back of her mind. She had become used to a life where she could not converse, and as the days passed, this seemed to trouble her only rarely. But all the while, somewhere in the back of her mind, she knew that she was desperately hungry to have her voice. She was most aware of this when Betty was talking about Mistress Mary, or if the Mistress herself was with them. Yet afterwards the awareness seemed to disperse, and she would carry on through the days, nodding and smiling, humming, and sometimes gasping when especially pleased. And no one complained about her lack of conversation.

Soon after Molly arrived at Betty's that day, Betty declared that she had a severe ache in her head, and she had taken to her bed, leaving Molly stitching alone. This left Molly with time for reflection, and her thoughts took her back to those hands. She shuddered and glanced over her shoulder, only to see the blank wall behind her. She wished that Betty were here, with her companionship and bursts of chatter. Yet although she trusted Betty well, Molly knew that she did not ever want her to know.

Then an alarming idea somehow wormed its way into Molly's mind. Could it be than in order to speak again, she would first have to tell what she knew of this monster? Nay, nay, that must not be the case. Molly hurriedly pushed all thought of it away. Yet soon it came again, worming its way back into her mind. Her body grew cold, and she picked up her shawl, and tied it securely round her shoulders. But this served only to increase her disturbance, as she remembered how her shawl had slipped from a shoulder that night, leaving the beast access to her bare skin.

Molly suddenly felt faint, and she swayed about in her seat. She put on one side the cloth upon which she had been working, and put her head low between her knees, just as she had seen the doctor instruct someone in a state such as hers. This steadied her, as it not only helped her state, but also reminded her of the reassuring presence of the doctor and her mother, and she was able to pick up her work again.

The doctor had been like a father to her. He had rejoiced in her good health, and had taken much interest in her every achievement. He had given her mother a room, and Molly had shared it with her from birth. She had known no other sleeping place. It was from that room that she had moved to the one that Sam, James and Alec had built for her and Sam to share.

What would the doctor and her mother say about her situation? Together they had cared for her, and saw that she came to no harm. Perhaps it was a good thing that they had passed away and were at peace, as they had been spared the knowledge with which Molly now struggled. But another part of her longed for their presence, and as this grew in her mind, she began to wonder if they had had some knowledge of this dreadful thing. If, as she believed, she had known it before, then surely at *that* time they must still have been alive? This last thought troubled Molly greatly. Her mother and the doctor had known everything about her. If a terrible thing had happened to her when they were alive, they *must* have known it, and if that were the case, why was it that they never spoke of it?

Molly longed for Betty to return to their workroom, but there was no immediate hope of this, as she could hear no sound of movement, and she guessed that Betty must have fallen asleep. She searched in the bag of scraps and pulled out a fragment of the beautiful lace, which she placed on the seat of Betty's chair. But although Molly could feast her eyes on the fine tracery of its pattern, its presence could not disperse the horrors that lingered in her mind.

Molly's thoughts returned to the doctor and her mother. It was inconceivable that they would not have spoken to her of some terrible happening that had involved her. But had this indeed been the case? Her mind could not absorb this new notion. It was surely impossible, she told herself firmly. But this determination did not serve to dispel her dilemma, and she was left with the awareness of the distinct possibility that her mother and the doctor had together decided to keep her in ignorance of something that had threatened her very life.

Then a new and very present worry gripped her. Betty had been resting for a long time. Even for someone who had fallen asleep, much time had passed. Was something amiss? Should she go and see if Betty was all right? But she had never before entered Betty's bedchamber, and doing so would not be considered seemly.

Molly tried hard to concentrate on her stitching. Surely Betty would waken, and she would return directly, greatly restored? She became aware that she should soon feed Nathan, but she was not free to leave without Betty's permission.

Eventually her anxieties got the better of her, and she went in search of Betty. She stood for a few minutes, listening intently outside the door of her bedchamber. Then, with trembling hand, she pushed at the door. It moved a little, but she could not see inside the room, so she pushed it again. It opened fully without a sound, revealing Betty stretched out on her bed, motionless and fully clothed.

Molly battled to remain calm, but her mind could not bear what her eyes had revealed to her. Her physical eyes informed her that this was Betty, but...

Molly could hear screaming – terrible screaming that went on and on. She wondered where it could be coming from, as Betty was asleep, and she herself could make no sound. Yet there it was. And now Betty was awake, and looking shocked, staring at Molly. Then she reached out to Molly...

When Molly opened her eyes, she could see something moving around quite close to her face, but at first she had no idea what it was. Then it became clearer, and she realised that it was Betty.

'Don't tell!' Molly choked out in strangled tones. 'Betty, don't tell!'

'There, there, dear,' Betty soothed. 'You had a bit of a fright, and then fainted. I expect when you saw me lying there, you thought something was wrong.'

But even to Molly's muddled brain, Betty did not sound convincing. She shut her eyes again, and took in a deep breath.

'I will fetch you a sip of water,' Betty told her, and Molly could hear her footsteps as she went to the kitchen. Instinctively, she put a hand to her forehead, as if to check its condition.

The sudden proximity of Betty's voice startled her. ''Ere you are. Take it slowly.'

Molly found to her surprise that she could sit up, and she leaned against the foot of the bed for support while she sipped from the cup that Betty handed to her. After that she felt steadier, and made as if to stand.

'Wait a while,' Betty advised. 'I can send word to Liza.'

Then Molly remembered that her son had to be fed. 'Nathan!' she burst out.

Betty's aching head had mended, but the ache been replaced with a muddle of feelings as she reacted to several greatly startling events. Molly had screamed – a piercing sound, enough to waken the dead. Then Molly had spoken, and not just once. Aye, Molly had spoken twice.

'Wait a while,' Betty repeated.

Molly felt weary, and she obeyed Betty's instruction without protest. Nathan was in good hands, and she would soon recover and be able to run quickly to feed him.

Betty went outside and sat on her stool at the door for a few minutes with her eyes shut, breathing in the air. The gentle breeze fanned her face, thus calming her and smoothing the furrows in her brow.

She was about to go back into her dwelling when Molly appeared beside her, looking more herself. Molly pointed in the direction of Liza's cottage.

'Would that my knees could take me as fast as you can run, and I would gladly come with you,' said Betty.

Molly touched Betty's arm lightly, shook her head briefly, and hurried to the gate, from where she set off at fast run. She was glad to have these moments to herself. Much as she felt safe with Betty, she needed to be alone. She knew that this day she had spoken to Betty, and she knew that she had spoken to her twice. What was it that had led to this? Such a thing had not happened since the brothers had found her as if dead. She recalled how Betty had left her alone that morning, needing to rest her aching head. At first this had not been a trial, but as time had passed, she had missed her companionship greatly. Then she remembered how this had changed to a feeling of alarm, and she had gone to find her.

Molly stopped in her tracks. She clutched at her throat. In her mind's eye, she could see Betty lying on the bed, not moving. She felt faint, and greatly unsteady on her feet, and it was as if she could not breathe. Then with the inner eyes of a distant memory, an image came to her, and she perceived herself as a small child lying on the ground, motionless.

'Mother!' she wailed.

The sound of her voice startled her back from that place, and she gazed around anxiously to see if anyone had witnessed her distress. There was no one in sight, and Molly ran again, arriving at Liza's cottage soon afterwards.

When Molly left, Betty had allowed herself a few more minutes at the door before going to the workroom and taking up her sewing. As she stitched, her mind again went over what had taken place in front of her very eyes. At first she vowed to tell Sam when he came for Molly later that day, but then she remembered that Molly had asked her not to tell. 'Don't tell. Betty, don't tell.' Aye, those had been her words. Although Betty's impulse was to tell Sam everything, instinct told her to at least delay such action. Aye, this must remain a secret between herself and Molly for some while yet.

Betty had had to keep plenty of secrets in her life. She was not by nature one who held things back, but necessity had often required this of her, and she was skilled in guarding private matters. She was certain that Mistress Mary knew this of her, otherwise she would never have confided so deeply.

Betty wondered if hereabouts anyone but she knew of Molly's father. Mrs Lark had one day confided a little of him, but only in the strictest confidence, and Betty had never breathed a word since. He had been a fine strong man, the only child of a blacksmith. He had met Molly's mother when away from home visiting distant relatives. He had straight away pledged himself to her, but when his father had found out, he had flown into a terrible rage, and father and son never spoke again. The son had had to leave the village of his birth forever. That place was called... Here Betty's memory defeated her. She tried again to find the name. Mort... Aye, that's how it began. But try as she might, she could not recall it. Lark had not been the man's name. Mrs Lark had been wed before she met him, but she had told Betty nothing of the circumstances. Mrs Lark had been unclear in her account of the untimely death of her beloved. All Betty knew for certain was that his death had led to Mrs Lark's arrival in the village, and her taking up her post at the doctor's house. Thank goodness she had, because without her, her own dear Jane might have been lost.

Sometimes Betty had been tempted to speak to Molly of what she knew about her father, but she had always held her tongue, remembering the solemn promise that she had made to Mrs Lark.

Betty stitched on. She told herself that Molly would be all right. She had appeared much restored by the time she had left for Liza's, and she would be there now, feeding Nathan. If Liza noticed anything amiss, she would surely tempt Molly to rest a little until she was steady enough to return here.

Yet as time passed, Betty found that she felt anxiety growing inside her, and she went to the door to look for Molly's return. There was no one in sight, and she again sat on her stool for a while. What should she say to Molly about what had taken place today? The answer to this question was not clear, and Betty was in a state of uncertainty about it. What should she do for the best?

Betty looked again in the direction of Liza's cottage, and this time she was sure that she could see Molly in the distance. Greatly relieved, she decided that she would wait for her return, and then divine how to approach her about the events of today. She went to her workroom and resumed her stitching.

It was but few minutes later that Molly appeared. Her cheeks were glowing, and she seemed fully restored.

Betty smiled. 'Nathan would be well pleased to see his mother.'

Molly nodded, seated herself, and began stitching.

Betty bided her time.

After a while, she said, 'I wonder if I should tell Sam what happened here today.'

Molly dropped her work onto her knee in alarm. 'Nay, nay!' she exclaimed.

'Hush, now. I was only thinking.'

But Betty's words did not reassure Molly. She was still greatly agitated, and burst out, 'Don't tell! Betty, don't tell.'

Yet again, those very words, Betty observed silently. Aloud she said, 'Molly, if 'tis your wish, I will abide by it.'

Molly looked as if she were wrestling with something inside herself, and Betty sought to put her mind at ease. 'I do not breathe a word of the Mistress' secrets to any living soul. Molly, I swear I will not divulge what happened here today.'

At this, Molly's expression changed. She grew quiet, and resumed her work. Inside herself she felt a great disturbance, but she did not want to show it. She longed for more time alone, so that she could think about what was happening to her. Her next chance would be when she ran to feed Nathan again.

Then Betty spoke. 'The hour for eating is long past.'

Surprised, Molly looked up from her work, and realised that until now she had had no thought of food.

Betty went on. 'The farrier took his meat with him. I will boil up some broth and call to you when 'tis done.'

This afforded a little time for Molly's thoughts to wander. She had spoken to Betty since her return from feeding Nathan. How could it be that she had spoken yet again today? She had been alarmed, but that could not be the only cause, as for more than a year such feeling had not led to this. But in her heart she knew that this day's alarm had been very different. It had come from a sight that had filled her with such sudden torment, and it had tried her sorely.

Then Betty called to her, and together they sat in the kitchen taking the hot broth.

'Molly,' said Betty, 'today you spoke my name.'

Molly kept her face down towards her soup. She nodded mutely.

'You have twice spoken my name before,' Betty told her carefully.

Molly dropped her spoon, and her broth splashed the table. Panicking, she drew in a quick breath. Confusion took over her mind, and tears sprang into her eyes.

For a moment Betty feared that she was causing Molly's state, but instinct told her that was not the case, and she persisted. 'The first time was when I hurt my finger on my needle, and the second was last summer, when I had fallen asleep on my stool.'

Molly felt as if a thick fog had pervaded her mind, making clear thought impossible, and yet Betty's words had parted the blanket, and had let beams of light through it. Molly clung onto that light. She could hear Betty's voice again.

'Both times you were worried about me, and today you were greatly alarmed at the state in which you found me. I think that each time you have feared something worse than what was there.'

The fog in Molly's head thinned. She wanted to fill her mind with what Betty was saying. She could hear the words, but as yet could not entirely grasp their meaning. She knew that she had spoken before. The brothers had talked of it. Now she wanted her own knowledge of it, and Betty was giving her this chance. Aye, that was it.

Betty could see that Molly seemed almost able to take in what she was telling her. On impulse, she rose to her feet.

'Come with me a moment,' Betty told her.

Molly stood up and obediently followed her. Betty led her to her bedchamber, and then took her hand and led her to her pillow.

'Lift it,' Betty encouraged gently.

Molly stared at her with a puzzled expression, but she did as directed, and thus revealed the peg dolls that lay beneath. She turned an enquiring gaze towards Betty, who then explained.

'I made them many months ago. 'Twas some time after you spoke my name for the second time. See, this one is of you before you can speak, and the other is of you with your voice restored.'

Molly could see that the first was draped with sadness, whereas the second was smiling, and her clothing was of bright hues.

Betty looked about her as if to search for unwanted presences. Then she whispered, 'I wove a good spell.' She paused before asking, 'Do you want to know the words?'

Molly nodded vigorously.

Betty drew herself up and took in a breath, before casting aside all caution and saying, 'Wickedness be gone. Let Molly's voice be mended.'

Betty could see that Molly looked very pleased. She herself was proud of the words that she had devised and had repeated every night, and she said, 'Shall I speak them again?' And without waiting for any further sign from Molly, she repeated her spell, savouring each word as she did so.

Then Betty replaced the pillow and said briskly, 'Come now. The broth grows cold.' She was certain that she had done the right thing in taking Molly into her confidence about the spell. Now it was time to replenish their energies, and resume their work.

Molly took a cloth and cleared up the mess that she had made, while Betty, with a voice like the contented clucking of a hen, expressed the opinion that in any case the table had been needing a good scrub. They finished eating their broth, and then returned to work.

Molly was greatly affected by the knowledge of Betty's spell. Betty was more than a teacher. She was a true friend, and she was as a mother.

As she stitched, Molly went over in her mind what Betty had told her about having called her name before, many months ago. Aye, she could remember it now. And seeing the blood on Betty's finger had brought back distant memories of her mother helping those who came to the doctor's house, covering their wounds when the doctor was engaged elsewhere. It was as if she could hear again the kindness in her mother's voice as she tended them. She longed to be as good a woman as her dear mother had been.

Then her mind returned to the day when the news of her mother's death had come. A neighbour had been sent to inform her, and she had gone to the village directly, but it had been as she had been told. Her mother was already dead. The good doctor had passed away not a year before, but before his end came, he had had the foresight to arrange a small cottage for her mother to have as her own. Her mother had missed the doctor greatly, but had delighted in her new dwelling, and had often sat at the door in the sun. It was there that she had been discovered, slumped forward, but supported by the wall behind her so that she had not fallen to the ground. When Molly had seen Betty appearing thus, she had straight away feared the worst. And now she had clear memory of having called out her name.

Something else began to form in her mind. What is it? Molly wondered. Yet as soon as she thought she had it, it faded, leaving only a faint shadow behind. But that shadow did not disappear, and later it took a more distinct form, as if about to reveal its complete nature, before fading once again to a state in which it was barely perceptible. Molly's best efforts to identify it were thwarted by its elusive nature, and her endeavours to push it away were confounded by its ability, despite everything, to remain somewhere in her awareness. Frustrated, she tried to concentrate all her energies entirely upon her stitching, but a resonance of the shadow seemed to appear even there.

Ah! Now she had it! But it was as a mouse that had evaded the hunter cat's most calculated leap, disappearing from sight, but hiding somewhere close by.

All this time, Betty herself was engrossed in her sewing, and seemed content to keep her own counsel, thus leaving Molly ample time for reflection.

More time passed, and as her sewing took a satisfying form, Molly fancied that what had been evading her full awareness was something that had been spoken, not by herself, but by another. Aye, that was it... Heartened by this step forward, she put her mind to discovering whose voice it had been, silently rehearsing the names of everyone she knew. Sam, James, Alec, Betty, Liza... She stopped. Betty! It had been Betty's voice, and she must have spoken something of importance.

At last she had it! Betty's words came back to her as if she had only just now spoken them. *You can speak, but you think you cannot.* Molly knew that today her situation had changed. Although she could not yet speak at will, she knew that she had spoken. She had remembered how, when concerned about her, she had called Betty's name twice before. And now she became certain about a future full of conversation. She did not know when that time would come, but it would, of that she was entirely sure. A smile spread across her face as she imagined Sam's joy at the discovery of this, and the happiness and laughter that would daily fill the cottage that they shared with James and Alec.

It was late in the morning when James departed. He planned to show himself around the village, and pass the time of day with whoever he encountered. He was in good spirits, and as he strode down the track to the road, he whistled a merry tune. The day had begun as overcast, and there had been a light shower, but now he could feel the heat of the sun penetrating through his shirt.

He encountered a stray dog, picking over some carrion. Next he saw a boy in ragged clothing, playing with small stones outside a badly-kept cottage. As his eye skimmed the building, he knew that inside would not be dry, as the roof appeared sorely in need of attention. As he turned a corner, he came upon a group of men who were talking in loud voices about the condition of the village well. James recognised some of them who worked at the quarry. He greeted them as he passed by, but they barely recognised him, so intent were they on their purpose. Two toothless old women sat in a doorway, deep in conversation. He called to them, but they seemed not to hear him, and he passed on. By this time he was near the house where the doctor had lived. It was now inhabited by a man who had made much money as a merchant. He and his large family filled the house. James had heard at the quarry that they lived a very simple life, eking out the riches that the merchant had formerly acquired. The small church where Sam and Molly had married was not much further on. He remembered that happy day as if it had been only yesterday. And here was the inn. The innkeeper was resting in the sun. His cap had slipped down over his eyes, and James could not see if he slept. The inn possessed a room where weary travellers could sleep the night away, but it was rare that any such person passed this way.

James walked slowly to the other side of the village, and then gradually retraced his steps. The innkeeper was awake by then, and James stopped and sat on the ground nearby.

'Seen any strangers in these parts?' James asked.

'None, except you,' came the reply.

James laughed loudly. 'I know you well. I am James, brother of Sam and Alec.'

'James!' exclaimed the innkeeper, and he slapped James hard on the back. 'You are much changed. I thought you to be a gamekeeper from the Master's land.'

'We work long hours for the Master, but not for that purpose,' James told him. 'Since we completed our cottage, he asked us to build for him. So content is he with our work that he will employ us for many a long year.'

'Ah, I had heard from some that there was a big man watching over them at the quarry.'

James smiled. 'I am he.'

'An' so 'twas you and your brothers that repaired the Master's house?'

'Aye, that we did.'

James was surprised that the innkeeper had not known all this already, but then he thought he might be checking that what he had heard was true. James himself knew well the need to know the truth of a tale.

'Know you a place by the name of Mortbridge?' he asked.

'I know it not myself,' the innkeeper replied, 'but I have heard tell of it. A dismal place by all accounts. There are dwellings falling into ruin. I cannot recommend it.'

'I will take good heed of your advice,' James told him. He stood up. He wanted to divine more, but he knew it was not wise to question the innkeeper further. To do so would be bound to attract attention. He had already said enough.

'Good day,' he called over his shoulder as he strode off.

By the time he was leaving the village, word had gone round that he was there, and several quarrymen sought him out to pass the time of day. James was pleased by this, and lingered a while. But he did not stay long. He would return next Sunday.

As James walked back to the cottage, he was well-satisfied with what he had achieved. Not only had he been seen by many, but also he had elicited information about Mortbridge.

When Sam spied James, he had to struggle to keep a rein upon his impatience. Endeavouring not to break into a run, he strode down to meet him.

'How went it?' he asked.

James smiled. 'My presence there has begun well.'

Sam wanted to shake his brother, but he stayed his hand. ''Tis too soon to have news,' he stated carefully.

'Aye, but I have some word of Mortbridge.'

Sam clenched his teeth tightly. He wanted to shout the name, but instead he stayed quiet as they walked abreast of one another.

'The innkeeper had heard tell 'tis a dismal place, with much falling into ruin. I could not ask more, as I feared he would perceive my interest as remarkable.'

'You did well, brother,' said Sam. He felt calmed. Although none of the questions that seethed inside him could be answered, he had a fragment of knowledge of the place that might lead him to what he sought. 'You did well,' he repeated.

'And I will return,' James promised.

Together they saw no need for Molly to know anything more of Mortbridge yet, but pledged to inform Alec.

The following morning, James arrived early at the quarry. Without knowing why, he had had a notion that he should arrive before any of the men were there, and because of it he had crossed the moor alone that day. The unusual lack of noise was almost eery. A great brown bird passed low overhead, and dived upon its invisible prey, before gliding off with it clutched in its talons.

James set about checking the wagons. They were constantly in heavy usage, and if one foundered, much time was lost. Thus employed, he became less aware of his surroundings, and was startled by the sudden sound of a man approaching. He looked up, and saw the young man who had last given him the instruction about a stone at the cottage. The young man hurried to his side, and made as if he were aiding with some small repair.

'I heard tell you were enquiring about Mortbridge,' he began.

James nodded.

'Did you not know 'tis an accursed place?'

James was immediately alert. 'The innkeeper did not tell me that, but only that it was part-ruined.'

The young man glanced back along the track before saying, 'Since the devil's work was done there, nought has prospered.' He dropped his voice to a whisper and added, 'No man should go there alone.'

Despite the spring warmth of the sun on his back in this sheltered spot, James felt a chill come over him, and he shivered.

The young man noted this and said grimly, 'And such would be the least of it.'

James was about to ask more, when he noticed the arrival of another, and when he recognised him as the very man who had questioned Nathan's ancestry, he quickly trod upon the young man's foot and fell silent.

Straight away the young man understood the meaning of this action, and he asked a question about the wheel of the cart upon which they worked. This was a good ploy indeed, as the man came to them swiftly. He addressed James directly, pressing him for more work at the barn.

'That I cannot arrange,' James told him. 'There is a rotation.'

The man persisted. 'I can speak to those who should go today. If one agrees, I could take his place.'

James could see the flaw in this arrangement. The man was one of the strongest, and no other would wish to challenge him. He calculated that he himself could beat him in a fight, but not without some kind of injury. He stroked his beard thoughtfully, as if considering the request. He was afraid that so great was his desire, this man might plan injury to be inflicted on another secretly, so as to take his place.

'You work well at the barn,' he stated.

At this the man appeared greatly pleased, and James could see that he thought his request to have been granted.

James continued. 'And you work well here.'

The man's face changed a little, but did not fall.

'Your presence in both tasks is equally valued.'

The man was clearly flattered by this, and he drew himself up, appearing taller for it.

'We sorely need your hands here these days, but as soon as we can spare you, I promise to send you to the barn.'

The man appeared satisfied with this, and he moved away and began to work with vigour. James completed the feigned repair, and soon went to labour alongside the man, pronouncing that they made a good team, and that he would seek him out the next morning when he was here.

In this way, an hour or two passed. Then the man could contain himself no longer.

'Why did you ask of Mortbridge?' he demanded.

James was ready for this question, as from the outset he had guessed that the man had wanted to talk of it to Thomas that morning.

'Ah,' he replied, as if taking the man into his confidence, 'that was a lure. I have need to find some way of drawing on the innkeeper's knowledge. He must know much of hereabouts. I began with a question to which I needed no particular answer. My real purpose is more obscure.'

The rhythm of the man's actions did not waver, but his tone changed.

'I know more than he,' he bragged. 'Although I am fewer in years, I am greater in many other things.'

James exercised great caution, as he knew that this man could not be trusted with anything but the quality of his labours. 'I am glad to hear this. I will try you with my questions, but can I trust you not to spread them about?'

'Aye, that you can.' The man paused, and then asked craftily, 'Why your lack of interest in Mortbridge? 'Tis a place full of intrigue.'

'I do not doubt that,' James replied. 'I know much of the place, but 'tis of no consequence to my greater purpose.' James was not a man to utter lies, and this statement was no exception. His true purpose was for Molly to have her voice back, and the story of whatever had taken place at Mortbridge was merely a piece of history to him. That history might have to be known, but it may also prove to be unnecessary to know it.

The man seemed well-satisfied with this reply, and asked, 'What answers do you seek?'

Then James began to toy in a cunning way with the man's interests and his vanity.

'I have assessed your labours many times, and have found nothing to be lacking. 'Tis true that you are a man of unusual skill and strength. I have oft reasoned that there must be much good blood in your forebears, but as yet I have no knowledge of them. Would you be willing to divulge your secrets?'

The man drew closer, and James could see that he narrowed his eyes.

'I have much to tell. But how would this be of benefit to you?'

James realised that the man was not as gullible as he had hoped, but he proceeded smoothly with his reply. Lowering his voice, he said, 'You must not breathe a word of this, lest it cause disturbance amongst the workers, or indeed in my family.'

The man spat into the dust. 'I can hold my tongue.'

'I must have a son, and I have long thought that I must find a wife for myself for that very purpose,' James lied. This time he could not tell himself that he was not dissembling, as he knew well that he was, but it was crucial that he lured this man away from the truth. 'My son must come only from good stock. Mortbridge has none, and will never be of interest to me. Know you of villages hereabouts that can supply such a woman for me?'

James could see that the man was immediately consumed with the purpose of becoming his relation by marriage. He had long divined that this man envied his position with the Master, and however distant the married relationship might be, it would make no matter, as the issue of the result would mean a sharing of blood.

'I will think on it,' the man replied. Then he added with a knowing look, 'You seek a goodly maiden, well-sired. I know much about my ancestry, and have many relatives hereabouts. I will come to you with the results of my searches. We will surely find a suitable match.'

James felt a sense of revulsion, but contrived not to let it appear in his voice, saying, 'I am indebted to you.' He knew that this was exactly what the man wanted to hear. Now he would have to count the hours until he could tell the others everything that had taken place that morning. He would have to include Molly in this confidence, as it would be alarming for her to hear his 'secret plan' from other lips. He planned to tell Sam, Alec and Thomas at the barn, once the two selected quarrymen had finished for the day, and he could then leave Sam to tell Molly on their way from Betty's to Liza's cottage. Sam would first have to inform Molly of what little he had learned about Mortbridge that Sunday.

Once the quarrymen had left the barn, the brothers and Thomas gathered at the rocks where they could look out for anyone who might spy on them.

The others were silent as James told his tale.

When he had finished, Sam said, 'I greatly admire your skill. I would not have been able to achieve this. 'Tis likely that I would have been overcome with rage instead.'

'Brother, it took much of my strength to conceal mine,' James assured him with a wry smile.

'I too have something to tell,' said Thomas quietly.

Sam's breathing almost ceased, so desperate was he that Thomas revealed what he had before withheld.

Thomas began. ''Tis about the young man at the quarry.'

At this, Sam's disappointment was so overwhelming that he almost began to rage at his friend, but he knew only too well the urgent need for constraint, and he made no sound.

'He is a distant cousin of mine,' Thomas explained. 'His grandfather was brother to my grandmother.'

Sam's attention was engaged immediately by this information. 'Why did you not say this before?'

'It is crucial that we never speak directly. Anyone who knew of our relationship might let the knowledge slip out in some comment or action. He and I are similar, but if we are not seen together, the similarity is not sufficient to attract attention. Sam, he knows the way across country to Mortbridge, and could be your companion. At this time of year, when the days are long, you could travel there by night and return the next.'

Sam grabbed Thomas warmly by the shoulders. 'No one need know of our absence if we leave after our work ends on Saturday, and return through the night that follows.'

Thomas nodded. 'You must wait until the month of June. The greatest light is at that time.'

'I will begin preparations. How can I communicate with the young man?'

'I have already alerted him to your need. From now on, James must be your messenger. The name of my cousin is Will.'

When Sam collected Molly from Betty's house, they were barely a few yards away when he began to speak to her.

Molly instantly took his arm, and put a finger to her lips to show him the need to quieten his tone. She felt a stab of annoyance when she learned that the brothers had kept the news of Mortbridge from her, but this faded as Sam progressed the story of the day's events, and it was soon replaced by a rising excitement that matched her feelings about the Mistress' secrets.

That very day, Betty had informed her that they were to go again to the Master's house to see Mistress Mary. Betty guessed that on this occasion the Mistress wanted to employ the privacy and secrecy of her own room, particularly after the alarm that affected her last visit. She had no doubt that the Mistress enjoyed her cups of camomile tea greatly. Perhaps she should take some of the dried herb with her, and leave it in the kitchens? But Betty discarded that idea. The Mistress would come again to her door, of that she had no doubt.

Molly looked forward to the next day with great anticipation of what news it would bring. She longed dearly for more word of the suitor, but she thought it unlikely that she would hear more yet. She and Betty had long known that the betrothal would not after all be announced in June. Yet now, with Sam's news, Molly knew that a different event would take place, one which concerned her own life, and had to be conducted in complete secrecy.

Molly and Sam had by now arrived at Liza's cottage, and they found her inside, feeding some oat gruel to Nathan to stem his hunger.

Sam watched Molly very closely that evening, but all he saw was a woman who was filled with happiness and gaiety. She had taken exceedingly well to his news, and so there was no impediment to his planning his journey to Mortbridge. Soon he would decide upon a date, and James would pass that information to Will.

Chapter Twenty-five

Molly was awake very early, as soon as the dawn broke. She lay quietly next to Sam, feeling his chest rise and fall. The birds were choosing their mates, and their songs filled the air. Soon nesting sites would be chosen, and a great variety of materials gathered. Molly thought of the cockerel that the brothers had recently added to their enclosure, and she looked forward to the prospect of the hens producing their own chickens, thus swelling their numbers. But today she was filled with the anticipation of attending Mistress Mary at the Master's house. Again she had tended her nails to make them smooth, and Betty had promised to lend her a clean apron. Betty had expressed anxiety about her capacity to walk the distance to the Master's house, and Molly had reminded her that she could bring two sticks, as a servant would be sent to carry the dress. As she lay there, a new thought came into Molly's head. She could carry a stool for Betty to rest upon if her knees troubled her greatly.

Molly must have fallen into a doze, because the next she knew was that Sam was sitting beside her, with Nathan in his arms. He gazed into her eyes, and handed their child to her.

When Sam left Molly at Betty's house, Molly could see that Betty appeared quite agitated. Assuming that it was because of her anxiety about her knees, Molly went through a number of gestures that indicated her plan about the stool.

Betty patted her arm, saying, 'Bless you, Molly. That will help me greatly, but there is another matter of which I must speak.' At this her agitation increased, and she began to wring her hands. 'Molly, I have a shocking tale to tell.'

Molly could not think what was distressing Betty so sorely. She started her stitching, and waited.

'When the farrier came in last night, he brought news that had been passed by someone from the village.' Betty took a deep breath, and then burst out, 'It concerns your James.' She looked closely at Molly for signs of disturbance, and seeing none, she continued carefully. 'He heard that James is looking for a wife.'

A slow smile spread across Molly's face, and Betty stared at her, bemused.

So, the quarryman had already used his loose tongue, thought Molly. She put down her sewing, and shook her head very deliberately. Then she put a finger to her lips.

'But 'tis true!' Betty was indignant. 'My own husband would not lie.'

Molly tried again. This time Betty attempted to grapple with the meaning of what she saw. She was certain that Molly was not disturbed by the news, and if it were true, she surely would be. But Betty stuck to her belief about the farrier. He was a man who might arrange to forget what he had heard, but what he remembered was always accurate, and he would never lie. Then a sudden thought struck her. Could it be that a tale had been put about?

Betty looked straight at Molly. 'Is this story false?'

Molly smiled and nodded.

'Ah! But for what purpose?' Betty questioned herself aloud. 'Such a tale is indeed a mischief.'

Molly wished from the bottom of her heart that she could explain to Betty what had been done, and why it had been necessary, but she had no means by which she could, and she resumed her work. Maybe she could later signal to Sam to tell Betty of it? But first they must make ready and go to visit Mistress Mary.

As if reading Molly's last thought, Betty threw up her hands and cried, 'Mercy! The time is passing! We must pack up the grey dress, and make ourselves ready. The servant will surely come soon.'

She and Molly hastened to pack the dress, and Molly placed it near the door. Then Betty carefully folded the black shawl and aprons, and concealed them under a cloth in a basket for Molly to carry. Molly put on the clean apron that Betty had provided, and then fetched the sticks for her. The servant arrived soon after, and left directly with the dress. Molly picked up a stool and the basket, and she and Betty began to make their way towards the Master's house.

When Betty first rested gratefully on the stool, she declared, 'What a fortunate invention! Molly, you have a sharp mind.'

Again, Betty and Molly were given food in the kitchen, and then they waited to be called to see the Mistress.

Once they were in Mistress Mary's chamber, she dismissed her maid and took them into the small dressing room.

'The sound of my voice will not carry far from here,' she told them quietly. 'Molly, bring a chair, and lay the dress out on it for me to see.'

Obediently and willingly, Molly followed these instructions. The dress was on the bed, still in its wrapping. She took out the pins that secured it, and arranged it on the chair.

The Mistress drew in her breath sharply. 'Oh!' she exclaimed. ''Tis a garment of exceeding great beauty.'

Betty spoke respectfully. 'I am glad you perceive it thus. May we help you to put it on?'

Mistress Mary gave a small shiver of excitement as she gave them permission to remove her black dress, and put the grey in its place. Then Molly brought the large mirror across.

'Mistress Mary, we have brought something that we hope will please you,' said Betty. She turned to Molly. 'I will steady the mirror, if you fetch the basket.'

Molly responded with alacrity. She removed the covering and took out one of the black aprons, which she tied round the Mistress' waist. Then she produced the fine black shawl, and placed it on her shoulders.

'We reckoned you needed something between the black and the grey,' Betty explained. 'That way there can be no criticism.'

At this, Mistress Mary turned and threw her arms round first Betty and then Molly, exclaiming, 'Most trusted and faithful helpers! I promise you shall have the foremost place in all things for my wardrobe. You will never want for orders.'

Betty flushed, and leaned on the back of the chair.

'Please be seated,' the Mistress instructed.

Betty gratefully lowered herself onto the chair, and rubbed her knees.

'My suitor will surely be greatly impressed when he next catches sight of me,' Mistress Mary declared, as she gazed at herself in the mirror. 'I had feared that the extended time of mourning would cool his ardour, but that cannot be the case now. I have this exquisite clothing, and now that a year has passed, he can at times visit this house with others to dine with us, and I can converse with him at such gatherings.' She clutched her hands together delightedly in front of her breast as she contemplated the future. ''Twill indeed be a happy time for us. Betty, can you and Molly complete the second grey dress with great speed?'

'We will do our best for you, Mistress,' Betty replied.

'I will not ask you to remove this dress for me. I should like to wear it,' said the Mistress, smoothing its skirts in a caress.

Molly noted this, and she shared silently in her Mistress' happiness.

Mistress Mary continued. 'Please leave by the kitchens. I have arranged a parcel of good things for your basket.'

Betty and Molly backed out of the room, and made their way to find Cook.

'Take it carefully. There's honey an' salt an' butter, an' there's eggs in there too,' Cook warned.

Molly retrieved Betty's stool and sticks, and together they made their way back to Betty's house, where she flopped down on her chair in the workroom, and fanned herself with a spare piece of material.

'Molly, you'd best run to feed Nathan, while I lie down and rest awhile. An' don't you get yourself upset if I fall asleep again.'

When Molly later arrived back, she indeed found Betty sleeping. She moved quietly into the workroom, and began to prepare more of the grey cloth. Her mind was full of the visit to the Master's house, and the imminent attendance of Mistress Mary's suitor. Surely his presence would be presented merely as one of several guests, and above all he would have to conceal his passion. But such effort would reap a rich harvest, as he would be able to converse quite freely with the Mistress upon every other subject, while drinking in her beauty.

Chapter Twenty-six

By the time the brothers gathered outside their dwelling on the evening of Saturday, James had made contact again with Will, the young man at the quarry. It had been but a short exchange of words, passed while loading stones into a cart, but it had been sufficient. An agreement was made that the journey to Mortbridge would be undertaken as close to mid-summer as possible, and that James would soon give Will the exact day.

This time, Sam made no move to exclude Molly from their meeting, and as soon as Nathan was settled, she came to join them.

Sam spoke first. 'On that day, we will all return here as would be expected, but directly after that, I will skirt round the village to keep out of view of prying eyes, and will meet Will near the milestone on the other side of it. I will hide in the nearby thicket and watch out for him. After that we will make haste in the direction of Mortbridge.'

'At all times you must watch out for danger,' James warned him.

'That I will,' said Sam.

'How will you enter Mortbridge?' asked Alec.

'I cannot tell,' Sam replied, and then went on. 'We know what we seek, but that cannot at first be found by searching the ground. It can be gathered only by searching the minds of people, and that is an uncertain task.'

At this point Molly pulled at Sam's shirt, and picked up a stick. She led him to a patch of bare dry earth not far from the cottage, and began to draw. Curious, the brothers stood and watched.

As the picture took shape, Sam could see that it was Betty's house, with Betty seated on her stool at the door. Molly drew another stool, and indicated that Sam was to sit on it.

'You want me to talk to Betty?' he asked.

Molly nodded her head, and drew another picture. This time, it depicted three figures beside a house, and they were watching another leaving.

''Tis me leaving for Mortbridge,' Sam pronounced.

Again Molly nodded. Then she pointed to the picture of Betty.

'Do you want me to tell Betty about it?' asked Sam.

167

Molly nodded very vigorously.

The brothers considered this request.

'Would that be wise?' James questioned.

Alec shook his head worriedly. 'This secret must be closely guarded. Can Betty be trusted?'

At this, Molly became angry, and she shook her finger at Alec, as if admonishing him.

Sam became thoughtful. 'Molly is well-accustomed to Betty's ways, and she would not ask this if she thought there was danger in it.'

'Aye,' James agreed. 'That is true.'

'Then I will speak to her very soon,' Sam decided. He saw straight away that Molly was content with this. Her demeanour was much changed, and she took him warmly by the hand.

James' visit to the village the following day was pleasant. When he arrived there, the villagers were already looking out for his arrival. Visits from those who lived outside the village were uncommon, while visits from strangers were rare. Stray dogs followed him, people called to him from their doorways, and the innkeeper was wide awake, watching out for him. He encountered many quarrymen, though not the one who had already spread the tale about him. It seemed that the spreading of the tale had worked to his advantage. It must be that with news of a forthcoming pairing, the villagers were already welcoming him back into their midst.

James felt saddened by the need for this deception, but the greater cause required it, and for now it did no harm. No maid could yet have been picked, and he hoped to be able to correct the tale before such a person's hopes were raised.

Again he dallied with the innkeeper, but this time enquired about his health, about the future care of the village well, and about the wellbeing of the occupants of the cottage that Mrs Lark had inhabited.

After this, he went to see the well, and then returned home by first passing back through the village.

True to his promise, Sam spoke to Betty that very Monday. When he arrived at her house with Molly and Nathan, he asked her if she would sit with him for a while at the end of the day. Betty agreed with alacrity. She knew that not only would she find conversation with Sam to be greatly entertaining, but also straightaway she sensed that there was something of import to be passed between them.

This arranged, Molly hurried off to take Nathan to Liza, and Sam strode in the direction of the barn. Although the work there was now far advanced, this was no time to slow their efforts. As soon as it was complete, they would begin the second row of cottages.

The early evening found Betty and Sam seated outside, on either side of the door of her house.

''Tis already the last week in May,' Betty remarked. She had on her lap a pocket-handkerchief, the corner of which she stitched with initials, intricately intertwined.

'You are making a pretty design,' Sam commented.

''Tis for the Master,' Betty explained. She handed the handkerchief to Sam so that he could examine it.

'Aye, I see it now.' Sam handed it back.

A few flies were circling the air close by, and one landed on Sam's hand. Deftly, he killed it with a single blow.

Betty admired this. 'My husband also has that skill.' She slapped her face where a fly had landed, but succeeded only in reddening her skin. The fly circled again, and settled on her nose.

Sam took the rag that hung in his belt. 'Stay!' he advised. Then by creeping up on it from the side, he grabbed the fly and crushed it.

'Mercy!' Betty exclaimed, greatly impressed. 'You have a cunning hand.'

'Aye, and 'tis of great help to me at other times.' Sam looked at Betty with meaning in his gaze, and their conversation deepened. 'Betty, Molly has persuaded me that I should speak to you of my planned endeavour.' He made a play of scanning the horizon, holding his hand above his eyes to shade them from the bright evening sun.

Betty concentrated her attention carefully upon her stitching. She barely moved her lips when she replied, 'You have my attention.'

'You must tell no one.'

'My lips are sealed.'

Sam paused, before saying, 'You know of a village by the name of Mortbridge?'

Betty was so astonished at this question that she almost dropped her sewing. Had Sam looked into her most secret thoughts? Surely not. Such ability was rare, even amongst older people, and in someone of his age and position, it was almost unknown. Yet he had certainly spoken the name of the place where Molly's father had died.

She answered carefully. 'Er... Aye, I have heard that name.'

Feigning some ignorance, she added, 'Ah, so 'tis a village?'

'Aye. 'Tis at a distance from here. I am to travel there soon.'

Betty searched her mind for something to say, but she was at a loss, and merely grunted. Sam was not deterred by this. He seemed not to have noticed her lack of response.

'Aye, near mid-summer's night.'

'That is indeed soon,' Betty commented. 'Will Molly and Nathan go with you?'

'Nay, 'tis man's work. I will travel by night with one other. No one must know.'

'I will not breathe any of this to a living soul,' Betty promised.

'A man from the quarry will come with me. His name is Will. He is well-acquainted with the route that does not follow the road. This will save many hours' travel, and we will watch over each other.'

'What is your business there?' Betty asked carefully.

Throughout this exchange, Sam had kept up his pretence of gazing into the horizon. He spoke only in a low voice, while Betty continued with her stitching.

Now Sam dropped his voice to a mere whisper. 'We have recently learned that Molly's father died in that place.'

Betty froze. How did Sam know this? She wanted desperately to insist that he told her the answer, but if she did he would surely guess that she had knowledge of her own, and then she would be tempted to betray Mrs Lark's trust.

Sam did not need to be pressed. 'A quarryman with a loose tongue showed a devilish interest in Nathan's ancestry. We have worked close by him, and have gleaned this much.' Sam was tempted to say nothing more, but he knew that he must trust Betty with the rest. 'Betty, rumour has it that Molly's father was killed by someone with the same blood.'

Betty could not prevent a gasp from escaping her mouth. She had put a hand up to still it, but it was too late.

'It cannot be!' she protested. But what she had heard did not sound at all impossible. It fitted well with what Mrs Lark had told her. She wondered if Sam knew of the smith, and of his rage on learning of his son's pledge to Mrs Lark. If indeed it had been the smith who had killed Molly's father, it was small wonder that Mrs Lark had not wanted to divulge this. Molly's father killed by her grandfather? This was too horrible an eventuality to contemplate, and yet it might explain everything. Betty clung tightly to the pocket-handkerchief in an attempt to steady herself. Aye, if Molly's father had been the only child of the smith, then he would have been expected to replace the smith in his old age. For him to pledge himself to a woman who had been married to another would have been too much for his father to bear, and in a moment of rage, father had killed son, in a desperate attempt to keep his house free from disrepute. The smith would surely have been a great strong man. All those who did such work had to be.

Sam had struggled to tell this much to Betty, and he had been glad of her silence. The outraged response that had come from her had confirmed his own reaction when he was first told, and he felt comforted by it.

At last he said, 'I have more to say.'

Betty glanced sideways at him. She did not know if she could bear what she was about to hear. She had no forewarning of it, but it might be even more alarming. She wanted to beg Sam to leave her. What he had said thus far was more than enough for her to endure. Then her mind turned to Molly. Dear Molly had wanted Sam to speak to her. For Molly's sake she must not close her ears.

Sam continued. 'Thomas is our friend. We know that he watches Mistress Mary on behalf of her suitor.'

Betty could not bring herself to say anything. Hearing Mistress Mary's secret spoken from Sam's lips was disturbing, and she was determined not to hear her own voice confirm it.

As if comprehending her dilemma, Sam said, 'You need say nothing. Thomas himself told us, and we have come to trust him with our business. Will is a distant cousin of his.'

This eased Betty's mind a little, and she asked, 'Is there more?'

'Aye. You will no doubt have heard of James' plans for marriage?' Here Sam chuckled heartily. 'That is but a tale to put the loose-tongued quarryman off the scent. He had heard from the innkeeper that James had asked of Mortbridge, and thus had come perilously close to intruding on our purpose. James told him that he had merely asked in order to gain the innkeeper's ear, and that his true endeavour was to seek a lusty bride. He gave out that he would find a relative of the quarryman greatly favourable.'

'Ha!' Betty exclaimed. ''Tis a devious lure, but no doubt successful in its cleverness. Aye, some of it had already got back to me, but Molly convinced me of its real nature.'

Sam and Betty sat quietly for a while, enjoying the shared

knowledge of the success of James' ruse.

Then Betty asked, 'Does Molly know all of what you have told me?'

'Near all of it. Betty, you must not tell her of the rumour of murder. She does not know it, and it would be a cruel thing to inform her, lest it be false. If we can confirm it, then I will tell her. The journey to Mortbridge might reveal the truth.'

Betty was now sorely tempted to tell Sam what Mrs Lark had told her, but with great difficulty she held her tongue.

She was helped when Sam announced, 'The hour grows late. I must go to Molly and Nathan.' He stood up, took her hand, and was gone.

Betty gazed after him, her hands idle in her lap. The murder was surely true. What would befall Sam and Will when they reached Mortbridge?

When Sam reached Liza's cottage, Nathan was already asleep. As always, Liza was in cheerful humour. She did her utmost to persuade Sam and Molly that although May was nearly past, they should continue their arrangement at least through June, and she hoped that indeed it would last for the whole summer. So confident was Molly of Nathan's bond with Liza that she felt happiness about this proposal, and Sam could think of no objection. His decision depended on what he observed, and since Molly, Nathan and Liza had each showed much pleasure in the company of one another, he was eager to agree.

Chapter Twenty-seven

The next morning Betty and Molly continued their diligent stitching of the pieces of Mistress Mary's second grey dress. The increased swiftness of movement of their needles did nothing to affect adversely the quality of their work.

'My conversation with Sam was of great interest,' Betty remarked. She did not want Molly to know of her anxieties, and she tried hard to keep her voice steady. She forced a laugh. 'James' tale is greatly entertaining.'

Molly sensed that Betty was strained, but thought it better not to draw attention to it, and concentrated on her sewing.

Betty went on. 'He spoke to me of Thomas.'

Molly stopped her work, and smiled across to her.

''Tis a great relief that Sam and his brothers know of Thomas' place,' Betty added.

Molly could see that there was now a twinkle in Betty's eyes. Reassured, she resumed her stitching.

Betty said nothing more for a while, but then she began to talk of Sam's plan to journey to Mortbridge.

'Molly, it should not be that Sam has to travel so far to find out about the death of the man who gave you life,' she said carefully. Then she added briskly, 'Yet he will not be away from you for long, and I have an expectation that he will certainly glean something for his efforts.'

Betty's words filled Molly with such a longing. How many more weeks would it be before she herself could speak? If only she could talk to Betty about her private thoughts on this matter.

Betty turned away from talking further about the plan, and instead she spoke of a conversation she had had with Liza.

'She came by on Sunday, and I spoke with her at length. She told me that you will bide with her for many more weeks.'

Molly nodded excitedly.

Betty smiled at her happiness, and then continued. 'That will greatly aid our work for Mistress Mary. An' Molly, she made much of Nathan's progress, telling me many stories of his achievements.

She has great pride in his strength.'

Molly laid her work on her lap, and clapped.

'Aye,' said Betty, 'we all know he will grow into a good man with great strength and character.'

There was another silence, after which Betty remembered something else.

'Together we wondered who might know about the making of lace. She too could think of no one, but we will not forget that you want to learn. A chance may yet come.'

That same day, a servant was sent to the barn with a message from the Master. He spoke to Sam. Afterwards Sam was jubilant. He longed for the day to end, so that he could tell the news to James and Alec.

As soon as the quarrymen left, he quickly approached them. 'I am told that a black heifer calf is ours. She is but a few weeks old, and is growing well. The Master's offer is to keep her till she is near grown, and then put her to one of his bulls.'

James was greatly excited. '’Tis certain proof of his intention to keep us in his employ.' Although he had never doubted the Master's decision to keep them as his builders, this was an added assurance. Wages in kind of such value were given rarely, and only to trusted workers of great skill and integrity.

Alec smiled broadly. 'I will visit her soon. She will still be with her mother, and I would like to see her qualities. I will enquire about her sire. I know that the Master shares bulls with certain neighbouring farms. We might have good blood from another source.'

Thomas joined them. 'Ah, you speak of your calf.'

'Why did you not inform us?' demanded James good-naturedly.

'The news was only certain last evening,' Thomas explained.

'Then you are forgiven for your tardiness,' Sam told him with a teasing smile.

Thomas turned to Alec. 'I think you are right about her sire. I am nigh-certain that he belongs to one who is greatly close to the Master's confidences.'

Sam was perplexed. 'Thomas, you speak in riddles.'

'Aye,' James agreed. 'Make it more plain.'

'That I cannot, but before the day is out, you will have divined the answer,' Thomas told them with a knowing expression.

When next together at their cottage, the brothers had many serious discussions about mid-summer, since that time was fast approaching, and with it the journey that Sam and Will were to undertake. By the time they left, the barn would be complete, and the new row of cottages begun.

They decided that James would continue his visits to the village. He need not seek any information, but his presence there would confirm the tale that the quarryman had spread, and when the time came for Sam to leave, it would aid the task of keeping his movements secret.

Still no one spoke of murder in Molly's presence, but that horror was always in the brothers' minds.

When at last the day came for Sam to leave, the signs were good. There had been no rain for more than a week, and so the ground underfoot was dry and firm. The heat of the day lingered on, but was softened by a lively breeze. He took little with him. Dry food and a good knife was all he needed. If seen by chance by a villager, nothing of note would be visible as he passed.

At the moment of parting, Alec insisted on following him at a distance as he skirted the village, to ensure that he reached the milestone safely and found Will. James stayed at the cottage so that he could guard Molly and Nathan.

As he passed the village at a safe distance, Sam encountered no one, and quickly reached the milestone. He concealed himself in the thicket, and waited. Alec had positioned himself on a hillock some distance away, from which he had a good view all round. It was not long before Will came into sight. He was strolling along the road, gazing around as he went, as if he had no particular purpose in mind, except to take in the air.

When Sam spied him, he whistled to him from the thicket. Will was instantly alert. He knew the sound of that bird very well, and it was not one that would be found singing in such a place. Will sat on the milestone, appearing as one who was resting. After covertly watching in each direction, he bolted swiftly into the low trees, thus disappearing from view.

'Ho!' whispered Sam. 'Your arrival has been long-awaited.'

Will was about to challenge this when he saw the smile on Sam's face, and instead he put a hand out to him. Then together they melted silently through the undergrowth.

When Alec had observed the arrival and disappearance of Will, he lingered a little longer. Seeing nothing further, he ran back to the cottage, and reported everything to James and Molly.

Liza had told Molly that Nathan had slept many hours that day. This suited their purpose well, as he was awake until late into the evening, thus providing endless distraction. James and Alec played with him, passing him back and to, carrying him around outside, imitating his sounds, and so making him laugh. Molly watched them willingly. Nothing would take from her mind the image of Sam striding across land unknown to him towards the place of her father's death, but the sight of James and Alec attending to Nathan warmed her greatly, so that she did not pine for him. But she prayed that Thomas' cousin Will would guide him safely, and she guessed that she and James and Alec would rest little that night.

Chapter Twenty-eight

Sam and Will passed few words between them, as Will guided them across the trackless heath.

'How know you the way?' asked Sam, bemused by Will's confidence.

'There are many signs,' Will replied. 'At this time of year, the sun's rays touch certain rocks, and reveal the shape of the hills in particular ways.'

Sam wished that he could learn Will's craft, but he knew that his life was with Molly and Nathan. He was a builder, and his eye was tuned for foundations, walls and roofs.

They moved almost silently, and from time to time, a solitary hare would bolt, almost from underneath their feet, and the birds of the heath would rise up, alarmed, deserting their nests, only to return again when danger was past.

As they travelled, they did not slacken their pace, and neither of them had any need to pause and sit. The imperative that filled their minds was the necessity of reaching Mortbridge as soon as possible.

By nightfall, Will had found a sheltered overhang. The air was now cool, but not uncomfortably so, and they curled up together for what little warmth they needed. But they could not afford to tarry long, and Sam found Will shaking him awake when the first crack of light appeared.

They found a stream, and mixed up some of the oatmeal that they carried, washing it down with the pure-tasting water. Although alert to their purpose, Sam still felt drugged by sleep, and he splashed some of the water upon his face. This was to the great amusement of Will, who watched as Sam's eyes lost their tired glaze.

Although still very early in the morning, it was now broad daylight. In the next hours they passed through hilly country, and had to cross a river that despite the dry weather still roared through its rocky bed. Sam picked his way carefully across the boulders, and was nearly at the other side, when his foot slipped and he felt himself falling. Yet by some miracle he righted himself, avoiding a pool of deep swirling water. Will was following close behind, but his crossing was sure-footed.

'Before we return, I must find a sturdy staff,' Sam decided. 'If I fall I will not drown, but I have no wish to soak my clothing through.'

Will was laughing quietly. 'You had the appearance of a jester.'

'I am glad to have given you this entertainment,' Sam told him wryly, 'but I cannot offer to repeat it when we pass this way again.'

'You need not,' Will assured him, amusement covering his face, 'I will not forget it.' Then his expression became serious. 'Sam, in not more than two hours, we will have sight of Mortbridge. Once at that place, we must stop and prepare ourselves, for it will then take little time to reach it.'

Sam was aware of tension gathering in his body as he walked. The movement itself calmed him, but its direction took him step by step nearer to Mortbridge, the place where dear Molly's father had died, perhaps murdered by the hand of someone he knew so very well that he did not suspect him until it was too late. Will noted that Sam's face grew grim as they advanced.

Having nearly crossed the hills, they were travelling towards the head of a valley. When Sam observed its greatly verdant appearance, this at first lifted his spirits a little. It surely was a place for herdsmen to tend their sheep and cattle. There they would grow fat and strong, and would survive harsh winters, or be slaughtered to feed many. He fixed his gaze upon it, but could see neither man nor beast. Will led them into the valley, and they followed the course of the river that ran down it.

Gradually Sam became aware of the sound of roaring water, and the further they went, the louder it grew.

''Tis a waterfall,' Will told him. 'When we reach its edge, we will see Mortbridge. There we will sit to talk. Then we must find a way down a cliff, and will reach our destination.'

It was as Will had said. The two men sat on the edge of the cliff, watching the water pour down its face into the end of a lake below. The river, quite broadened, left the lake at the other end, and trailed away into the distance. Sam could see Mortbridge standing on the left side of the lake.

'Where was the bridge?' he asked.

'I believe it crossed the river at the other end of the lake, but a great flood in early spring one year swept it away, and there has been no one to rebuild it.'

Sam thought this to be strange, but said nothing. He could see a few buildings scattered on the green area to the right of the lake, which was curtained and cut off by very steep ground. Surely such a sheltered spot would be greatly prized, and men should have quickly built a new bridge? As he watched, he could see some animals grazing there, but he was not certain whether they were sheep or goats.

'To descend this cliff is perilous,' Will told him, 'but there is a way. Soon I will show you, but you must promise to do exactly as I tell you.'

Sam had no wish to risk harm to himself, and agreed straight away. After the journey through the night, he trusted Will's knowledge and skill completely.

Will went on. 'When we have made our descent, we must work our way through the buildings very slowly. The few people who still live here are old and weak, and are entirely unused to visitors of any kind. They will surely become alarmed, and cannot fly like birds or run away like the creatures of the heath. They need time to discover that we mean no harm.'

'I will watch you closely, and follow your every sign,' Sam promised.

At this, Will stood up and led him to an indent in the edge of the cliff. 'I will lead. Match closely my every move.'

Although a brave and strong man, Sam felt as if his heart was in his mouth as Will slowly guided him down that cliff face. There were several times when his body froze in fear, and he had to use all his inner determination to force it back into movement. And when at last they reached safe ground below, he found that he was shaking.

'You did well,' Will commented without expression. 'Now we will advance.'

Will turned and walked very slowly towards the first dwelling, with Sam following close behind. He realised that as they distanced themselves from the sound of the waterfall, everything was eerily quiet.

Then they disturbed a number of scraggy hens that instantly began to dash about in great alarm.

A cracked voice from an invisible form called, 'Who passes? Is it friend or foe?'

''Tis two friends,' Will answered, projecting his voice so that the hidden would hear.

A thin long-haired man scuttled from the first building. He

moved low to the ground with the aid of a rough crutch. Sam could see that he had only one leg, and he was clothed in rags.

'Who are ye?' the man demanded, looking frightened.

Putting a hand on Sam's shoulder, Will announced, 'A distant relation of my friend once lived here many years ago.'

This had the effect of provoking curiosity in the small man, and he crept forward towards them. Sam could see that he had no teeth, and that one eye had no sight at all.

The man peered at them, and then declared, 'Not foe.' He turned, and shouted as loudly as his creaking voice would allow, 'Not foe!'

At this, several heads appeared from behind walls and broken doors, and many pairs of eyes peered at them.

Will had made no attempt to advance further, and Sam did not question this.

'We carry nothing with us,' Will called, 'but we can offer you some hours' labour.'

Several of the partly-hidden people came out of their rotting havens, and clustered together in a tight group. It was difficult to see each individual, but Sam was sure that Will had been right. There were no children amongst them. All of them were bent, and few had any teeth. They were clothed in what Sam supposed were the remnants of garments, but he imagined that they must have lost their identity long ago, and they barely covered them. Apart from the first, each carried a stick, upon which walking depended. One began to cough, making a dry hacking noise and then spitting blood on the ground.

Sam wanted to run. He wanted to run to the cliff and scale it, back to the safety of the empty green valley, and then find his way home. He wanted to see Molly and Nathan. He wanted to see James and Alec and Thomas. This was certainly a terrible place. What could have befallen these poor people, who could barely scratch out an existence, and had only ruined buildings for shelter? Their houses were in a far worse state than he had imagined. And yet Sam knew that he had to stay. He had to find out what had happened to Molly's father.

Then he saw another inhabitant coming from the far end of the village. This person moved slowly, but without a stick. And as the form came closer, Sam could see that it was a woman. She looked no younger than the others, but her appearance was less ravaged by time and disease. The group moved to one side to let her pass.

'No one comes here by chance. You have come for a reason,' she stated.

'Aye, that is right,' Will replied, but he did not know what to say next.

Sam stepped forward. 'My wife's father died here,' he explained boldly. 'We have come to see his grave, and honour him.'

The woman considered this, and then asked, 'What is his name?'

'I know it not,' Sam replied. 'He died before my Molly was born, and she was raised by her mother in the house of the doctor in the village where I lived.'

'In that case we may not be able to help you,' the woman told him.

Sam thought quickly. Intuition told him that he should not yet give the name of Mrs Lark.

'Now that we are here, we can give a little help to you,' he said, confirming Will's earlier offer. 'I am a builder, and my friend is a quarryman.'

Again, intuition had warned him not to divulge their intention to leave that night.

'You offer great kindness,' answered the woman. 'As you can see, there is much here that we cannot attend to. The graveyard is beyond the village, and at a greater distance from the lake. You have our permission to visit it. If on the way you see something that you can repair, then you can stay here awhile. We have little to eat, but you can share what we have. There are rabbits nearby, and we snare them. There is other food, but it is not in our power to benefit from it. If you can reach it, you can take it. There are many fish in the water, but we can catch one only rarely. Ducks nest at the lake, but we cannot reach their eggs. Across the lake are goats, but since the bridge was swept away, we can no longer reach them. They survive well there, as the grass is good, and the shelter of the rocks sustains its growth for many months.'

'We are indebted to you,' said Will. 'My friend and I will approach the graveyard with respect. After that we will return to you with our offer.' He turned to Sam. 'Come, Sam, we must hurry. There is much to do.'

They walked quickly to the far end of the village, and from there could see the graveyard. Minutes later they were searching, but there was little to see, other than variously-shaped rocks and rough wooden crosses. There was nothing to show the names of the people who had been buried there.

Sam threw himself down on the grass beside one of the graves, and almost wept.

'There is no hope of furthering our quest,' he moaned. 'All has been in vain.'

'Nay, nay,' Will chided. 'We will rest here, and then we will make lines to catch fish, and we will collect eggs from the ducks.'

'But that will tell us nought of Molly's father,' Sam objected.

'When we feed the villagers, their tales might inform us,' Will pointed out quietly.

Sam sat bolt upright. 'Forgive me for my slothful mind, Will.'

'As Nathan's father, you are burdened by the need for urgent discovery of his grandfather's identity. I will help you all I can.'

Sam jumped to his feet. 'Come now. I am restored, and we must begin to hunt. There is food to catch and food to gather in, and that will bait the greater catch.'

Together they returned to the lake, and set about devising ways to trap the fish and collect the eggs. The villagers watched with great interest and anticipation. Sam and Will threw each fish to the waiting hands, which despite their age and some deformities, deftly gutted them ready for consumption, while others took the eggs, handling them as rare treasures.

'A feast,' said one.

'Aye, a feast,' replied another. 'We have not seen such food in years.'

'There is more here than we will need for these next days,' a third assessed.

'Smoke some fish,' advised another voice excitedly.

Others began to make ready a fire. Dead wood lay in plenty not too far a distance from their houses, and the ones who were less weak dragged branches to a site that was ringed with stones. There they arranged a rough frame on which the fish could be laid or hung.

'I must inspect the site of the former bridge,' Sam told Will. An idea had come to him, and he wanted to see whether or not it could be followed through.

'I will stay. The fish are collecting here to be gathered in,' Will replied cheerfully.

When Sam reached the far end of the lake, he examined the situation carefully. A simple bridge would allow the villagers to reach the goats again, and that would mean further sustenance. The addition of the precious nourishment provided by milk and the carcasses of male kids could transform their lives. But how could he provide such a structure when he had only a few short hours left in this place? He went back to Will.

'Will, I must endeavour to give these people a way to their goats,' he said in a low voice. He did not want to be overheard. The villagers must not know his intention, lest he was unable to honour it.

'I am of the same mind,' Will told him quietly, 'but I do not have the skill. Can you see how it might be achieved?'

'I have an idea of it,' Sam replied, 'but I will need to be here for several days.' He fell silent, and then added, 'If we do not return this night, the others will be sorely tormented.'

'Aye, 'tis true.'

'This work would give us more time to hear the tales of the villagers.'

'I am of the same mind.'

'Then shall we risk the effect upon those that we have left behind, and stay here awhile, trusting that they will believe in our safety?'

'We surely must.'

Their minds made up, Sam and Will redoubled their efforts to gather in as much food as they could, while the villagers smoked, cooked and stored whatever they received.

Long before the late dusk of the middle of summer, the friends were called to share the feast. Sam counted the heads of five and twenty people as he sat eating. Still no children had appeared, and there were no women here of childbearing years. The village would surely die out, but if he could help them, the inhabitants would be more likely to die only of old age, and not of starvation.

The villagers wisely ate but little, and very slowly, while Sam and Will did not need to take such precautions. Not only were they young and used to filling their bellies, but also they must replenish their energies ready for the hard day's work that would follow.

It was as they sat round that Sam let slip Mrs Lark's name. The woman who had given them permission to attend the graveyard was sitting near to him, and she immediately turned and enquired, 'How know you that name?'

''Tis the name of my dear Molly's mother,' Sam explained. He wished that his tongue had not become so loose, but it was too late, and now he must face the consequences.

He noticed that the woman's face looked even more pale than

before, and she struggled to speak. When she did, her voice was a whisper, and Sam had to lean towards her in order to hear what she said.

'I once heard her name.' She paused, and her struggle became greater. ''Twas from the blacksmith's son.'

Sam was relieved to see that no other seemed to have heard what she said, and he moved closer to her.

'There was a smith here?'

The woman nodded.

'He is no more?'

The woman nodded again. It was as if her voice had been stolen. This stark reminder of Molly's condition clutched at Sam's heart, but he was determined to persist.

'What kind of a man was he?' he asked.

The woman eyed him carefully, and then said, 'Bigger and stronger than you, and with massive hands.'

At this, Sam felt himself grow faint. He swayed against Will, who grabbed a cup of water and held it to his lips. By great good fortune, this action restored him almost immediately.

'What troubles ye?' Will enquired.

'Come,' said Sam abruptly. He stood up, touched the woman's arm kindly, and left the circle with Will.

They backed away into the growing gloom.

'We have to stay here,' said Sam urgently. 'The blacksmith is dead, but I just heard tell that he had massive hands, and the woman told me that his son once spoke Mrs Lark's name. Will, I can barely speak. Go now, and tell them that I will stay and make a crossing to their goats. You can return to the others and inform them.'

'I will announce your intention, but I will not leave you here alone,' said Will.

Sam glared at him in the dark, but he knew that Will's resolve would not be shaken, and he said no more.

They returned to the circle, and Will stood in the middle, at the side of the fire. The villagers fell silent.

'My friend and I have been talking,' he began. 'We will do our utmost to construct a crossing to your goats. We cannot promise sure success, but you will have our best efforts.'

Then Sam stood beside him. 'I plan to divide the flow of the river, and bridge it in sections. Tomorrow Will and I will begin work. If there are any amongst you that can roll rocks and bring timber, then come. Now we must sleep.'

Soon Sam and Will were curled up together in a corner of an abandoned building, and they fell into a deep slumber almost instantly.

The next morning, all the villagers had gathered at the end of the lake when Sam and Will went to begin work. Even the weakest were there, intent on doing what little they could. Sam took off all but his leggings, and waded into the river. The dryness of the last weeks had much reduced its level, and this aided him greatly, since it enabled the foundation of his broad rock pillars to be laid with least interference. Taking into account the great flows of water that were to be expected when ice and snow melted in the spring of each year, he began to divide the river into four sections, increasing its width greatly, but ensuring that its depth would never be able to carry off the structures that he planned. He worked with hardly a break. Throughout this tireless devotion, he thought only of the future of these people, some of whom must have known the father of his dear Molly. His mind could not yet accommodate thoughts of the blacksmith, except to liken him to the devil himself.

That evening, as everyone again ate together, Sam emptied his mind of the reason why he had come, and instead concentrated on his plans for the following day. Will made no attempt to remind him. His concern for these good people was as strong as Sam's, and he knew that their first purpose must wait until the building work was complete.

Already benefiting a little from additional food, some villagers were able to work in pairs and in threes, shifting rocks, and others began to fashion lines and wicker traps for fish, as they had seen Sam and Will use. Yet others rolled stones from the more collapsed buildings with the intention of making small platforms along the edge of the lake, from which they could temporarily extend timber to gather eggs.

When Sam had not returned home on the morning of Monday, James and Alec set off across the moor carrying Nathan, with Molly beside them. Although they had hoped to see him by now, they felt little anxiety, believing that he would be back quite soon. There were many unforeseen things that could have delayed his return, and James and Alec reassured themselves that his absence did not herald bad news.

It helped them that Molly herself was happy and cheerful, showing no sign of distress.

James left Molly with Betty, telling her that Sam would soon be with them. He then hurried on to take Nathan to Liza. When she expressed surprise at his presence, he made a remark about Sam having been delayed. After that he strode away quickly to the quarry, with Liza gazing after him.

In the privacy of the small workroom, Betty chose her words with care. ''Tis not surprising that Sam has not yet returned. He undertook a journey of great purpose, and who knows what sources of help he has encountered.' Inwardly she hoped that he was already safely back at his dwelling, and had been so overcome by lack of sleep that he had lain down and fallen into a deep slumber. If that were the case, he would arrive here this very afternoon at the latest.

Molly found no difficulty in advancing her work. She knew in her heart that although Sam had not returned, the shared knowledge of his intent was a bond between them, and she felt sure that he must be safe. And this feeling did not fade as the day wore on and he did not appear, so that when James came to see her at the end of the day, she was quite calm. He said little to Betty, and then walked with Molly to Liza's house, where he stayed for the night. He asked Liza earnestly not to breathe a word of Sam's absence, and asking no questions, she agreed.

Betty herself had spent the day in a sense of rising panic that was mixed with curiously calm certainty, and hard though she tried, she could not make out the meaning of this. She made no mention of the situation when the farrier returned home, thus keeping it all to herself.

From that day on, it was James who came and went with Molly. He made no move to talk to Betty, except to pass the time of day, as there was nothing that he could say. Each day, he asked Liza to keep her own counsel about Sam's absence, and although not having any understanding of the position, she did not press for information. Instead she concentrated upon Nathan's wellbeing. The fact that Molly seemed unchanged reassured her greatly, and she determined to wait and see what transpired.

Each day Alec ran between their home and the construction that was to be the new row of cottages. This place was less far from their dwelling than was the barn, but only by a few minutes of Alec's speed. Every morning when he arrived, Thomas looked to him for news, but there was none to give. Every day, when James came,

Alec's face was tense with expectation, but he had to accept disappointment. James was able to report that Molly was in continued good spirits, and this sustained them.

Although Thomas himself could not understand the reason for the long delay in the return of Sam and Will, he had no fears about the situation. News would have been welcome, but it was not necessary to him. As one who was trusted completely by the Master, Thomas had passed word to him that Sam's return from a family matter had been delayed, and this had been sufficient explanation. The Master himself was not one for idle chatter, and Thomas knew that he would not remark on it to anyone. James had informed Thomas that he had devised a tale to spread at the quarry that would account for Will's absence, but since no one there had yet remarked upon it, he had said nothing. He supposed that the quarrymen were now so used to some of their number being temporarily employed elsewhere that they did not give it any conscious attention. With the completion of the barn, it was no longer the case that two men were sent there each week, and he kept one of the reserve villagers at the quarry to make up for Will's unobserved absence. He supposed that Will had informed his grandfather in advance of the venture that had taken him away, and that that wise man was diverting the attention of any village gossip away from such a subject. It was fortunate that the loose-tongued quarryman was so intent on finding him a wife that he too seemed to have observed nothing untoward.

Betty lay awake for much of each night, her mind turning over all of what she knew. How she wished that she had divulged to Sam everything that Mrs Lark had told her! She had been right to remain loyal to the trust that had been placed in her, and yet this course could have led Sam into meeting misfortune, and all because she had not warned him of her well-founded fears. But he must have known that he was facing great uncertainty, and he had a good companion. Betty could not have wanted for better than a cousin of Thomas.

By day Betty endeavoured to put her darkest fears aside for the sake of Molly, and she invented the kind of cheerful talking that was her ordinary habit. Molly's unchanged state was a puzzle to her, but it was also a relief. She herself had witnessed some of Molly's greatest distress, and she had no wish that Molly should be thus tried, but she could not fathom the reason for her apparent calm. Had the farrier been away without good reason, Betty was certain that she would not have been able to maintain her equanimity.

With each day that passed, many of the villagers of Mortbridge grew a little stronger, and their endeavours advanced. Sam's work continued successfully, and everyone began to comprehend what he intended the result to be. In the evenings, he would search amongst the deserted buildings to identify where the best beams could be had, as once his foundations were in place, these were crucial in the task of constructing ways of spanning the newly-devised sections of the river.

When the end of Saturday came, James and Alec together collected Nathan from Liza, and met Molly at Betty's door. There they did not linger, as they did not want anyone to note the absence of Sam in their midst. Liza had wisely asked them no questions, and Betty satisfied herself with but a smile and a wave to Nathan. Some weeks ago he had begun to recognise her without difficulty, and he liked to engage with her in this way.

They crossed the moor in silence, each hoping to find Sam waiting for them at their cottage. Yet when they arrived all was deserted. Molly set about feeding Nathan, and James and Alec sat down to assess the situation.

James' voice was grim. ''Tis a full week since he left here.'

'Aye,' replied Alec, 'and since I watched him reach the milestone.'

'What can be done?'

'I know not.'

The brothers fell silent for a while, and then James touched Alec on the shoulder. 'Come, we will cut wood.'

Knowing that there was no need for this, Alec almost resisted, but then he realised what his brother meant, and he went outside. They did not move far.

'Must we now tell Molly the rest?' asked James.

Alec shook his head. 'Not yet. There is still time for them to return.'

James was not convinced. 'Alec, I begin to lose heart,' he stated. 'I fear that some ill has befallen them.'

''Tis too soon to know that.'

Although James agreed, this was of no comfort to him. 'I cannot rest.'

'Rest does not come easily to me these last days,' Alec replied. 'But what of Molly? She seems well.'

'I am glad, but I cannot divine the reason for her state.'

Then James and Alec heard a footfall behind them, and they turned to see Molly there.

James spoke to her. 'Molly, there is still no sign or word of Sam.'

Molly nodded calmly.

'Should I set off now to search for news of him?' James enquired.

Molly shook her head emphatically.

James pressed her. 'Why not?'

Molly fetched a stick and began to scratch in the dry earth at their feet. First she drew two figures, one tall and broad, the other shorter and more slender.

'They are Sam and Will,' Alec guessed.

Molly nodded. Then she drew a number of small houses, and indicated that there was water nearby.

James was perplexed. Why had she done this? What had she depicted? Aloud he asked, 'A village?'

Molly nodded.

It was then that James knew. ''Tis Mortbridge.'

Molly pointed to the figures, and then to the cluster of dwellings.

Alec was filled with astonishment. 'You know they are there?'

Molly smiled and nodded. She endeavoured to make James and Alec smile, too, but having not succeeded, she began to draw again. This time, James was certain that she indicated a lake, with a river running from it. Then she gathered a handful of small stones, putting some at each hand of the figures, and then pointing to where the river left the lake.

James was truly amazed, and he exclaimed, 'And you know what they are doing! Molly, what is this magic?'

Molly pointed to the side of her head, then to her eyes, and then to her head again.

'You can see them inside your head, but not with your eyes?' Alec guessed.

Molly smiled, and clapped her hands.

James turned to Alec. 'I have heard of such a skill, but I have never yet known someone who has it. Are we to believe this?'

At this, Molly showed anger, and made a play of striking James across his buttocks. Alec was relieved to see that James took this in good humour, twisting round and plucking Molly off her feet, holding her high in the air. She feigned to beat him on the head, but with silent laughter and gaiety, until James put her down again.

'How many more days must we wait?' asked Alec seriously.

With mute concentration, Molly counted the fingers of one hand, but when she turned to the other, she could not be certain.

'So 'twill be at least five more days, and beyond that you cannot tell?' said Alec.

Molly became subdued. She wanted to know the answer to his question, but it was not clear.

'Maybe it cannot yet be certain,' James suggested.

At this the worry fell away from Molly's face, and he knew that he had the true meaning of her fingered response.

'Alec, tomorrow I will go to the village as before,' James announced.

'Then I will stay here with Molly and Nathan, and I will not move from them.'

When Sunday came, Sam and Will did not pause from their labours. Each day was the same to them, a dedication to the villagers. There were occasions when the memory of their quest came into Sam's mind, but he thrust it away vigorously. The time would come when he would consider all of it, but that time was not yet nigh. Will said nothing more about the subject, and Sam did not need to ask in order to know that he was of the same mind and purpose.

By the end of Wednesday that week, two great timbers and some long iron bars spanned each of the gaps between the stone foundations, thus making four rough bridges. Sam and Will secured the ends of these with more rocks, and then watched as the first villager crossed the river dry-footed. The man made his way straight to the first of the scattered dwellings on the other side, and disappeared inside it, emerging only minutes later with a skin in each hand. Slowly and cautiously, several others crossed after him, while the less firm waited uncertainly. Those who had crossed approached the other buildings and produced a number of items – signs of much dried grass, more skins, and various devices for fishing and trapping.

Sam and Alec joined them in order to assess the condition of the buildings, and they found them in a state of good repair, which they put down to the sheltered aspect of the situation. Then they worked to tether the goats.

That evening there was much rejoicing in Mortbridge, with a pitcher of goat's milk being passed round to drink to the health of Sam and Will. The villagers plied them with questions about what they might do in return, and it was then that Sam reminded them of why he and Will had come.

Then the woman to whom Sam had earlier spoken Mrs Lark's name stood up and said, 'You have given us back our strength. Together we will now be able to prepare for the winter. Without you, most of us would surely starve or freeze to death. Instead we will store food, and we will make two of our dwellings sound, so that we can gather together for warmth. While you have worked here, I have asked each person what they remember of the smith and his son. Those who were here at the time of the son's death are of one mind.' She beckoned to the man with the crutch to take her place, and then she seated herself on one side of Sam.

The little man spoke in his cracked voice, but in a way that Sam and Will could hear very clearly.

'The blacksmith was a great, huge man. I heard tell that the only thing he longed for in life was the birth of a son who could succeed him. His wish for a son was granted, but the birth took away the life of his wife, so his son remained his only child. He reared the boy himself on goat's milk and gruel, and when he was old enough, he began to teach him the ways of the smithy. He was a fine boy, who learned well. At the time, there were nearly two hundred people in this village, and there was plenty of work for the smith and his son to do. Those who heard of them from neighbouring villages were willing to make difficult journeys to come here for such help. Then came a day when the son wanted to go out into the world. His father gave him permission to go to a place where a distant relative resided, but he was to return in not more than three weeks. It was while he was away that he met Mrs Lark, and he loved her from the moment he set eyes on her. He knew that he had to spend the rest of his life with her, and he returned here only to let his father know this. When the smith heard it from him, he flew into an ugly rage, and with his huge hands he beat his son until the breath of life left him, declaring that his son would never have his permission to leave the village again. If his son's love had been a maiden, then he could have had her here to live, but because she had been already married, he could not tolerate such a liaison. The son was buried here, and I can show you where he is laid. The smith later learned that Mrs Lark had born a child, and he vowed to find that child and destroy it, saying that no blood of his son would live on in a child of such a woman. He disappeared from here for a month or two, and when he returned he was much changed. He spoke little, and was always morose. Some say that he had found the child, and had strangled her almost to death, but at the last moment had relented, because it was only a girl.'

Hearing this provoked extreme torture in every fragment of Sam's body. So, the smith had nearly killed his Molly before? The rage he felt about this defied description. It wanted only to fly about, and yet he knew that he must not let any of it out. Will quickly moved close to him, and leaned against him gently. It was as if Sam had made his body as a pillar of stone, lest he destroy everything within his reach.

Unaware of Sam's extreme distress, the man continued. 'From that day on, this village was doomed. Crops failed, fevers overcame us, women lost their babes, and infants died in arms. Only few people survived. Then the bridge collapsed in a great flood as the snows melted in the spring of five years ago, and separated us from our animals. No one has since come to make his home here, and those whom you see are the ones that have lived on.' Here the man paused.

'What happened to the smith?' Sam asked of him.

''Twas more than a year ago,' the man began, 'early in the month of December.' But here his voice faltered.

Sam knew that his hands were trembling, and he trapped them under his legs in an attempt to conceal it. He glanced at Will. His face was set, but if he felt any disturbance, he did not show it.

'Tell us,' Sam urged. But the man said no more, and he faded away behind some of the others.

The woman stood up again. 'I will take you now to his son's grave.' She turned, and Sam and Will followed her.

Sam was seething inside, and the cold black hatred that had lived inside him since the dreadful day when he had found his dear Molly for dead now threatened to fly loose. He *must* avenge what had been done to her. But how could he if he did not know where the smith had been laid?

Then he heard Will whisper in his ear. 'Think first of Molly's father.'

When they reached the graveyard, the woman pointed to a large stone that lay flat, saying, 'He is beneath.' After this, she left them, and Will could see her resting a short distance away.

Sam groaned and fell to his knees beside the stone. 'Here lies the father of our dear Molly, and grandfather of Nathan. I know not yet his name. Will, we must discover it so that we can scratch it here for others to see, and we can tell Molly of it when we see her again.'

After some time of silent vigil, Sam and Will approached the woman, who was still waiting.

'Tell me his name,' Sam asked.

'I have heard that his name is Nathan,' the woman replied.

This news punctured the darkness in Sam's heart. 'Ah, 'tis a worthy name. My youngest brother and my son are called by it. Tomorrow I will carve it on the stone for all to see – Nathan, son of the smith.'

'We would ask you not to do that,' said the woman urgently.

'Why is that?'

'We do not speak of the smith, and any evidence of his name would be unwelcome.'

Sam considered this request, and then asked, 'Well, then, what of his mother?'

'She was a daughter of a good herdsman. You may write "grandson of the goatherd".'

'That I will,' Sam agreed. ''Tis a pleasing solution.' He gathered himself. 'Now you must tell me of the smith's death. Once I know it, I will ask nothing more.'

The woman's face grew pale, and she looked as if she would fall to the ground, but she steadied herself by clinging to the rock on which she sat. Her voice was barely a whisper as she told the tale.

'One night at the start of the December before last, there was a terrible storm with thunder and lightning. The lightning struck the forge, but no one dared leave their homes to see what damage had taken place. When the storm abated, one or two crept up to see, and found the smith, scorched to death. We all believed that this was a just end to his evilness, and we vowed not to bury him in our graveyard, amongst the good souls who rested there. Instead we hacked his body to pieces, and burned them in the fire of the forge.' Here she bowed her head, as if in acknowledgement of the dreadfulness of their deed. 'We took the ashes, and strewed them as far from here as the strongest could travel, while the others tore the forge apart. But it made no difference to our plight, and we wonder if we have since been punished for our actions.'

'How could that be?' asked Sam gently. ''Twas in truth a cry for help. It could be that it was heard, and that is what has led us to you.'

The woman looked at him with gratitude. 'You put your own need to one side to help us in our plight. Your goodness will be well-rewarded.'

'At home we already have a kindly Master who values our work.

My wife has learned the art of a seamstress, and is in good favour with the Master's sister. My son blossoms. The only thing that is left to want for is to have my wife's voice back.'

'Does your wife not speak? Why is that?'

'Near the time of the death of your smith, she was sorely attacked, and was left for dead. Since that time, she has spoken only a few words.'

The woman made as if to speak, but Sam raised his hand to stay her, and went on.

'Until the man spoke this evening, I knew nothing of the evil that had been done to my Molly when she was a child, but by his description, it is as if that evil returned on that night.'

Then the woman stood up, and raising her face to the sky said, 'Wickedness be gone. Let Molly's voice be mended.' She turned to Sam. 'You have done everything you can to halt the ruin that descended on Mortbridge after the death of Nathan, grandson of the goatherd, and now I will do everything I can to help to restore your Molly's voice. Every night I will ask for this, and I will ask the others to do so too.'

Sam was greatly affected by this, and he said nothing more.

'The night is with us,' Will reminded them. 'Sam, you and I must sleep, and tomorrow we must return to our homes.'

Molly tossed and turned on her mattress in Liza's cottage. The air was still hot from the baking sun of that day, and her throat felt dry. She thought of rising to fetch some water, but she did not want to wake Nathan and James, who were sleeping close by her. Then she saw that James too was awake.

'My throat hurts,' she told him.

'I will fetch water for you.' James got up and brought a cupful from the pot that had cooled over the dead fire. His head felt muddled, and he could not clear his thoughts.

Molly spoke again. 'Sam and Will are safe.'

'That is good news indeed.'

It was then that James realised that he and Molly had been conversing, and he stared at her with incomprehension.

Molly seemed not to notice, and said, 'Thank you for the water. My throat feels better now.' Then she lay down, and fell asleep almost instantly.

James lay awake for a long time. In the silence he wondered if he had dreamed what had just passed, but he knew that he had not.

When he woke the next morning, Molly was already moving about with Liza and Nathan. When he spoke to her, she replied only in signs, and appeared to have no memory of what had happened in the night. Yet when they arrived at Betty's house, everything changed. Betty was waiting at the gate, and when she spied them coming, she hobbled to meet them.

'Molly! Molly!' she called. 'The dolls!' She seemed to care not that others might hear her.

Molly ran to her. 'What has happened?' she asked.

'Come and see,' Betty replied.

The two women hurried into the house, leaving James staring after them. He knew nothing of dolls, and now he had again heard Molly speak, this time to Betty. Confident that Molly was in good hands, James left to start work at the cottage row. He wished that Sam were here. Molly's confidence about his whereabouts and his safety had helped him, but he had never been parted from his brother for this length of time before, and it tried him sorely.

Inside the house, Betty explained. 'They were under my pillow when I went to bed early last night, but when I came into the workroom this morning, this is what I saw.'

She opened the door of the small room, and pointed. There were the dolls, lying on the chair where Molly always sat.

Molly touched her throat. 'Something has changed,' she said quietly.

At the cottage row, James went straight to Alec and Thomas.

'Something has changed,' he told them. 'Molly spoke to me last night. Her throat hurt, and I fetched water for her. Then she spoke again and fell asleep. This morning she was silent, but later I heard her call to Betty.'

'This is good news indeed,' said Alec excitedly. 'Could it be that Sam will be home soon?'

'That cannot be the only reason for her speaking,' James pointed out. 'But every day I long for his return.'

'You told me early this week that Molly seemed certain it would be only a few more days before Sam and Will were seen here again,' said Thomas.

'That is true,' James agreed. His longing to see his brother again, alive and well, was so strong that if he could have transported him here by magic, it would have been done.

Sam and Will had left Mortbridge as soon as they had woken. The villagers had bade them farewell, and had stood at the foot of the cliff, watching silently as they climbed the perilous route to the top. Then Sam and Will waved and went on their way, back up the empty valley towards the hills. They said little as they walked, and when at last they reached the river crossing, they sat and rested.

'You will need a staff to cross,' Will jested.

Sam pushed Will into a patch of heather, declaring that he had stood in cold water for over a week, and cared not if he fell in. Then he jumped to his feet, and bounded sure-footedly across the boulders.

There was no need for sleep on this journey, but from time to time they slowed their pace, and sat for a while, watching all that was around them. Sam knew that to hurry would not bring him any quicker to Molly, Nathan and his brothers. He aimed only to reach the cottage by the time James and Alec were there. But would they come? he wondered. Since he had not been there to stay beside Molly at Liza's cottage, perhaps James or Alec had done so. He would find out on his return.

It was late afternoon by the time they reached the thicket by the milestone outside the village. Sam and Will were loath to part. They had been together for a long time, and together had accomplished something momentous. That they were about to go their separate ways seemed wrong.

'Maybe in time you could find your way to our dwelling,' said Sam. ''Tis rare for anyone to come that way, and you would not be observed.'

'I will ask my grandfather for advice on it,' Will replied. 'He is wise in these things.'

Then the two men parted, Will to go to the village, and Sam skirting it to reach his dwelling. Sam arrived home without mishap, and could see from what he found that at least one of his brothers was sleeping there. He lay down on a mattress for a nap, and was soon sound asleep.

When Alec arrived later, he could see that the door had been disturbed, and he was immediately on the alert for danger. Stealthily he crept up to the door by sliding his back along the wall, and looked in. There he spied Sam asleep on his mattress. His face was a good colour, and he was breathing evenly.

Alec was overjoyed to find his brother here, alive and well. He wanted to take him in his arms, but equally he did not wish to wake him, so he sat watching him, immersed in the knowledge that Sam was home again.

It was a good time later when Sam woke. At first he did not know where he was, but then he saw Alec watching him, and he let out a great cry.

'My brother! 'Tis so long since I last saw you.'

Alec put a foot on Sam's chest. 'When I saw a stranger on my mattress, I nearly took out my knife,' he jested.

Sam grabbed Alec's leg and tugged hard at it, making his brother fall on top of him. There they wrestled for a while, laughing.

Aftewards Alec offered some boiled rabbit from the pot.

'I have been feasting on good fish these last days,' Sam told him. 'Mortbridge had a surfeit, though the villagers were too weak to catch them.'

'You must tell me all.'

Alec said very little else while Sam told the tale of his journey to Mortbridge. Then he described the descent of the cliff, the plight of the villagers, the gathering of food, the building of the new bridges, and finally the story of the blacksmith and his son.

'So,' said Alec, 'there is no doubt that murder was done.'

'No doubt at all.'

'And that it was the smith who killed his own son.'

'Aye.'

''Tis small wonder that the village fell into slow ruin after that.'

'Aye.'

'But why did the villagers not thrive again once the smith was dead and they had burned him to ashes?'

'They took away the ashes, and they destroyed the smithy, but they could not take away the wrong,' Sam explained. 'The death of the smith's son had to be honoured, and the damage the smith did to our Molly has to be mended.'

'I heard from James only today that Molly spoke last night to him, and again to Betty this morning,' Alec told him excitedly.

'Ah, so what the woman asked has had an effect!' Sam exclaimed.

'What say you?' asked Alec.

'The woman who helped us asked for the wickedness to be gone, and Molly's voice be mended.'

'But that was not all,' Alec pointed out. 'You honoured the Nathan that was Molly's birth father, and named him on his gravestone, and you had restored the bridge that had been swept away, thus leaving the villagers with hope.'

'And there is something else. The blacksmith was killed when he was struck down by lightning in his own smithy. From the description we were given, it could have been on the exact day when Molly was struck down in this very place.'

Alec was amazed by this revelation, and it was a long time before he spoke again.

'Sam, I cannot comprehend what this means.'

'Nor I,' Sam agreed. 'I am impatient to tell James and Thomas, to discover what they think, and I fancy that at the earliest opportunity I should tell everything to Betty.'

'If all is as I believe, you will be able to talk with Molly about this matter.'

Sam and Alec spoke until late into the night, and then they slept together, Alec on his mattress, and Sam on James'.

The next morning they rose early, and set off across the moor in time to see Molly, James and Nathan at Liza's cottage. Nathan was still sleeping when they arrived, but when Molly saw Sam, she ran to him, throwing her arms around him and holding him tight, while repeating his name over and over again.

'I knew that you would come soon,' she told him.

James stood and watched this with tears in his eyes. Although he wanted to ask Sam everything that had taken place since they were last together, he knew he could wait. The most important thing had happened – Sam had returned.

Liza watched over Nathan, waiting for his earliest move. Though she was in her own cottage, she did not feel it was her place to be here at this meeting, and all she could do was make sure that Nathan was brought into it in the kindest way.

At length, James took Sam's arm. 'I must go to the quarry, but I will join you at the cottage row after noon.'

'Watch over Will for me,' Sam asked.

'That I will,' James replied. Then he was gone.

Nathan woke, and Liza handed him to Sam. 'Nathan,' he murmured, 'I now know that as well as your connection with your uncle, you have taken your grandfather's worthy name, and I will tell stools at the door.

When they heard him, they looked up from their sewing, and Molly jumped up and ran to him. Hand in hand they returned, and Sam sat with them both to tell the parts of his story that he knew were easy to accept.

Throughout this account Molly sat quietly, never changing the pace of her stitching, whereas Betty could not contain herself, and would frequently mutter an exclamation, and at the same time would stitch all the faster.

Sam had hardly finished when Betty burst out, 'So 'tis certain dear Molly's father rests at Mortbridge.'

'Aye,' Sam assured her. 'That is the case. And I have made the inscription on his gravestone for all to see.'

Betty was greatly excited. 'An' his name was Nathan too.'

'Aye, Nathan, grandson of the goatherd.'

Molly looked at her husband. 'Now tell of the evil,' she instructed calmly.

'Er...'

'Sam you must tell it, and you must tell all of it,' she insisted.

Betty's hand flew to her mouth, and her sewing dropped on her lap.

Molly reached out a hand and placed it on Betty's knee. 'There is much more to tell.'

When he had first learned it at Mortbridge, the knowledge had been unbearable. When he had informed the others, it had been hard. But now, speaking of it to Molly seemed impossible. To tell her of the evil of her grandfather towards her father, his own son, was horrible to contemplate, but to tell of his vile actions towards her very self was something that he could not face. And yet this is what he had to do. Slowly and painfully Sam began. His brow ran with sweat as first he recounted the terrible tale of how Molly's father had met his end.

Despite his struggle with his own difficulties, Sam noticed that Betty was becoming more and more agitated, and he had barely finished speaking when she said, 'Sam, Mrs Lark hinted as much to me. I longed to warn you before you left for Mortbridge, but I had given her my solemn vow that I would never tell a soul.'

'What did my mother say to you?' asked Molly in the same quiet tones as she had employed before.

Betty seemed to freeze, but then she swallowed hard, and after that she began to speak. 'Molly, she told me that your father was a fine strong man, the only child of a blacksmith. He met her when he was away from home, visiting distant relatives. He straightaway pledged himself to her, but when his father found out, he had flown into a terrible rage, and father and son never spoke again. The son had to leave the village of his birth forever. She told me that Lark had not been his name, and that she had been married before, though she said nothing of the circumstances. Molly, I swear she did not tell me how your father died.'

'Thank you, Betty,' said Molly. 'I am certain that my dear mother would be glad that you have now told this.'

Sam stared first at Betty and then at Molly. How could he continue? But he must. He shut his eyes for a moment, and then went on, watching Molly and Betty carefully. Although Betty's stitching hand jerked a little from time to time, he could detect no other sign of disturbance.

When he had finished, he could see that Betty's face had turned quite pale, and it was Molly who spoke to him.

'Sam, I have known some of this before.'

His denial was instant. 'That cannot be!'

Molly continued. 'Betty has been a witness to some of it.'

Sam was astounded, but before he had time to speak, Molly went on.

'One day here, Betty had a severe ache in her head, and she went to lie in her chamber. As time passed, I became worried, and I went to find her. When I saw her lying there...'

At this, Betty took up the story. 'Your Molly screamed a terrible scream, and collapsed right on the floor of my bedchamber. It was a while before she opened her eyes again. Then she called out "Don't tell! Betty, don't tell". I gave her water. I wanted her to rest, but she was determined to run to feed Nathan. I could not hurry with her because of my knees.'

Molly touched Sam's arm. 'When I was going to Nathan, my throat felt strange, and suddenly I could see myself as a small child, lying on the ground, and I cried out for my mother. This must surely be a memory of the smith's attempt to kill me.'

Sam gazed into Molly's eyes. 'You have triumphed over his evil.'

Betty sat and watched them with tears in her eyes.

'Molly,' said Sam gently, 'I must also tell you that Thomas had

But Nathan would not have this. 'That is not enough of an answer,' he retorted angrily.

As had often been their way together, Sam reached out to pluck him off the ground as a kind of play, but Nathan ducked and twisted, and slipped from his grasp. Then he darted out of the door, and was gone.

Sam ran after him, but when he could see no sign of where he lay hidden, he gave up and returned to Molly's side.

'What think you?' he enquired.

'You have a hard task,' she replied, laughing. 'He has set his mind on it.'

'Would the thought of such an endeavour trouble you?'

Molly considered this for only a moment, before replying, 'I think it would not. Our son is ready to go out into the world with his father, and what better a journey to consider?'

'Midsummer is but two more weeks away.'

Molly would not be drawn, and merely nodded.

Sam fell silent. This time there would be no need for secrecy. They could leave early, travelling by day, and reaching Mortbridge many hours before sunset. He knew not what they would find. After the passage of these ten years, the people he and Will had known there may all have died. He must warn Nathan of this, as the child's mind might see the place only as it was in the story he had so often been told. Sleeping there for a single night would be sufficient. The next day he could show Nathan the graveyard. Then they could retrace their steps, and arrive back here before the day was done. If something unforeseen prevented them from leaving Mortbridge until the following day, then so be it.

There was still no sign of Nathan, and Sam went outside to call him in. There was no answering sound from him. No rustle, no breaking of a twig, only the call of the owl, as it hovered near the barn. Sam felt no worry. This had happened so many times before as to be commonplace, and he left him in the care of the warm twilight.

When Sam woke the next morning, he found that Nathan had crept onto the mattress behind him and had lodged himself there, though there was very little room for him. Sam found his son's hands in front of him, as in his sleep he had wrapped his arms round his father's chest to secure himself.

Sam tried to work his way off the mattress without disturbing him, but Nathan was awake in an instant.

'What is your answer?' he demanded.

Sam gave him a broad smile. 'I fancy we might attempt it,' he teased.

Nathan made as if to hit his father's chest, but Sam grabbed his fist to force a handshake.

'We will leave in two weeks' time,' he promised. 'The present task at the Master's house is well-nigh complete. I have no doubt that he will agree to spare me for two days after that.'

Nathan's happiness was complete. He ran to his mother with requests for food to carry with him, but she told him that now he was a man he should trap and gather at least some of it himself, and she would only supplement it if it became necessary.

At midsummer, Sam and Nathan left long before Molly and Lark were awake. When Sam took the route down to the village, Nathan prevented him, saying, 'Nay, father, you must show me the way that skirts it.'

Sam smiled indulgently, and acceded to this request.

Once at the milestone, Nathan touched it. 'The meeting place.'

The thicket had long grown into a dense wooded place.

'We will go round it,' Sam told him. Nathan was about to protest, but his father insisted. 'We must not risk poking an eye with a stick, or indeed tearing our clothes, when there is no need.'

The crossing of the heath was just as Nathan had imagined it. It was a wild place, much like the moor that he knew so well. He ran about amongst the heather and ferns, until Sam gave him a caution to use his energy well. They rested for a while before continuing to the river that was bedded with boulders. Sam watched Nathan carefully, as with agile leaps, he found a way across. Then Sam followed, taking good care. The water was higher than when he had last passed this way, and he had no wish to disrupt their journey by slipping into its swirling flow.

Sam gazed around to be certain of the way, but he remembered clearly how Will had shown him the unmarked path through the hills.

Some hours later, they rested in sight of the head of the green valley. It was there that Sam noted the first change. He was certain that what he could see was a flock of sheep grazing there. He turned to Nathan, but his son's sharp eyes had already made this out.

'Look, Father!' he said excitedly. 'The empty valley has filled

The Fifth Key by Mirabelle Maslin

ISBN 978–0–9558936–0–5   £7.99

Soon after Nicholas' thirteenth birthday, his great-uncle John reveals to him a secret – handed down through hundreds of years to the 'chosen one' in every second generation. John is very old. His house has long since fallen into disrepair, and as Nicholas begins to learn about the fifth key and the pledge, John falls ill. Facing these new challenges and helping to repair John's house, Nicholas begins to discover his maturing strengths.

The unexpected appearance of Jake, the traveller whom Nicholas has barely known as his much older brother, heralds a sequence of events that could never have been predicted, and a bond grows between the brothers that evolves beyond the struggles of their ancestors and of Jake's early life.

Order from your local bookshop, amazon.co.uk or the augurpress website at www.augurpress.com

Poetry Catchers by The Pupils of Craigton Primary

ISBN 978-0-9549551-9-9   £7.99

Craigton Primary is an inner-city school in Glasgow, Scotland.
has over 200 poetry-mad pupils, and it is the first school in Glasgo
to have its own poetry library!

All of us have written a poem for this wonderful book.

We have picked our favourite poems, and we hope that you enjoy readi
them as much as we have enjoyed writing them.

We have been inspired by Michael Rosen and our poetry-loving teach
Mrs McCay.

Some of the poems will bring a tear to your eye, and others will make y
cry with laughter.

Why don't you open the book and see what's inside?

**Order from your local bookshop, amazon, or from the Augur Press
website www.augurpress.com**

See also Kinship Ark Press

www.kinship-press.com

Printed in the United Kingdom by
Lightning Source UK Ltd., Milton Keynes
142168UK00001B/5/P